T0307999

ART DOES (NOT!) EXIST

ART DOES (NOT!) EXIST

BY

ROSALYN DREXLER

Normal

Published by FC2 with support given by the English
Department Unit for Contemporary Literature of Illinois
State University and the Illinois Arts Council

Address all inquiries to: FC2, c/o Unit for Contemporary
Literature, Campus Box 4241, Illinois State University,
Normal, IL 61790-4241

Art Does (Not!) Exist
Rosalyn Drexler

ISBN: Cloth, 0-932511-98-8, $19.95

Jacket design: Brian Pentecost
Book design: David Dean

Produced and printed in the United States of America

1

This book will help me decide which project to present for an NEA Fellowship in Visual Arts-Based Performance, Video, and new genres. At the moment my life is in flux. I'm doing nothing. How can I? My heavy equipment is in storage. I don't have a place to live. My funds are at an all time low. And my nutty husband wants me back. I'm thinking of putting myself in storage, but there's no lock on the inside. As Clov, one of Beckett's characters says in *Endgame*, (pause) "I can't be punished any more." He waited for the end of the play to leave. I'm already gone. What does it all mean?

THE MEANING OF LIFE

ONCE AS I STOOD UPON A HILL OBSERVING A STARLESS, INKY VISTA, IT WAS SUDDENLY REVEALED TO ME THAT LIFE WAS NOT A FOUNTAIN, BUT A FOUNTAIN PEN. I WAS AMAZED BECAUSE IT HAD NEVER OCCURRED TO ME THAT LIFE COULD BE A FOUNTAIN, MUCH LESS A FOUNTAIN PEN. IF ANYONE HAD BOTHERED TO ASK ME I WOULD HAVE TOLD THEM THAT LIFE IS MORE LIKELY TO BE A RUSTY U-SHAPED SEWAGE PIPE JOINING HEAVEN AND EARTH, SAME AS "NUT", A PRIMORDIAL GODDESS OF THE SKY WHOSE PROFOUND FEAT AL-LOWED THE SOULS OF THE DEAD TO ASCEND TO HEAVEN. AS FOR FOUNTAIN PENS, EVERYONE KNOWS THAT THEY ARE ERRONEOUSLY LABELED, BEING NEI-THER FOUNTAINS OF KNOWLEDGE NOR ANY OTHER KIND OF FOUNTAIN. IN THE HANDS OF GENIUS, OF COURSE, THEY CAN BESTOW ETERNAL LIFE—BUT ONLY TO WORDS. THIS IS THE TRUTH. ANYWAY, AS MOTHER GOOSE, MY REVERED #1 GURU, ONCE WROTE ON HER

ANCIENT COMPUTER:
    FOR EVERY EVIL
    UNDER THE SUN
    THERE IS A REMEDY
    OR THERE IS NONE
    IF THERE IS ONE
    SEEK TILL YE FIND IT
    IF THERE BE NONE
    WELL NEVER MIND IT.

MY SITUATION

I'M LOOKING FOR A CHEAP APARTMENT ON THE LOWER EAST SIDE (NYC). MY LIFESTYLE HAS BECOME SO ERRATIC (SOMETIMES I STAY UP ALL NIGHT EDITING TAPES OR WRITING) THAT I FIND IT IMPOSSIBLE TO LIVE WITH ANYONE ELSE OR TO SHARE AN APARTMENT. I NEED SPACE AND QUIET. SAFETY, FORGET IT. I WATCH MY ASS, NOTICE WHO'S AROUND. WHAT MORE CAN I DO?

EARLY SEX EDUCATION

PRESSED MY CUTOUT ONE-DIMENSIONAL PAPER DOLLS TOGETHER WHILE I MADE KISSING SOUNDS— AFTER WHICH I LET THEM SHARE EACH OTHERS' CLOTH- ING, AND SENT THEM (APPROPRIATELY ATTIRED) ON A WHIRLWIND TOUR OF THE CAPITALS OF THE WORLD. MY OWN LIFE HAS NOT BEEN PRIVY TO SUCH TRADITIONAL COURTSHIP RITUALS. AT THE AGE OF EIGHT I WAS GROPED UNDERWATER AT A CITY POOL. AT THE AGE OF NINE I WAS FONDLED BY A RELATIVE IN A SUITE AT THE WARWICK HOTEL. AT THE AGE OF TEN I SEDUCED AN OLDER COUSIN WHO LATER BECAME A BOTANIST. AT THE AGE OF ELEVEN I ABSTAINED, TOTALLY ABSORBED IN READING BALZAC. AT THE AGE OF TWELVE AN UNCLE PUT HIS TONGUE IN MY MOUTH. AT THE AGE OF THIRTEEN I HAD LUNCH AT AN ITALIAN RESTAURANT

8

WITH MY FAMILY DOCTOR WHO HAD BAD BREATH.
FOURTEEN AND UP, I DANCED IN THE PARK FOR PENNIES.
AT FIFTEEN I RETIRED.

COMMENT

I USED TO HAVE MORE FUN.

LOOKING FOR AN APARTMENT:
TIME TO GET SERIOUS

An ad in the Real Estate section of the Sunday Times describes what I am looking for: furnished apartment, low rent.... I call the landlord, make an appointment to see the place. It's not far from Chinatown, near SoHo. We meet in front of the building.

"You're on time," the landlord says, "shows you're a responsible person."

"Yeah I've been accused of that before."

I follow him down a few stone steps to the basement entrance. A rusted iron gate stands open. We go in. Takes a while for my eyes to adjust to the dark. What I make out is a large space divided by a column: I point to an empty space to the left of the column where one might put a bed, then to a small alcove over which a bare bulb hangs. The landlord pulls on the light cord and the dim 40-watt bulb flickers on then off again. The floor below the bulb is scraped, as if a heavy table had been dragged across it.

"Where's the table?" I ask the landlord. His name, Stan Baltimore, is on the card he hands me.

"You take the place I'll get you a table," he says, "maybe even a bed."

It occurs to me that Stan Baltimore would like to screw me. The way he says "bed." The way his hand brushes my arm when he talks. So what else is new; if I play along, flirt a little, maybe I can get him to give me a good deal on the place. It's not perfect, but it'll do.

INNER THOUGHTS
(unless otherwise designated, all dialogue with a Q or A before it, is to be understood as what I am thinking)
Q: Are you willing to sleep on a used mattress?
A: A used mattress can be dangerous territory, harboring bugs—stains of an intimate nature—unexpected protuberances — indentations—odors. A friend of mine (Juan Ferra) burns the mattresses he finds in empty lots in order to exhibit them as art. He calls his art: "Mattress World" (Not to be confused with Dial-A-Matres ((Leave off the second s for savings)). Juan devoutly believes that there is nothing, no matter how broken or dirty, that cannot not be reclaimed as art.

"But one has to be careful," he says, displaying a badly burned hand, "not to get too close—the work and the artist must remain separate: art can kill the artist as surely as the artist can kill the art."

GOD I'M TIRED. I'D BE BETTER OFF IN BED

Q: Have you inspected this apartment?
A: Why do you ask?
Q: Remember to run the water in the tap; washers wear out. Landlord should replace. Look for signs of illegal entry: chipped paint on the door jamb beside the lock. Is a dead bolt necessary? Where is the telephone jack? If there is none, will there be an additional charge for installation?

There are suspicious holes in the wall beside the door. Perhaps shots were fired...somehow connected to an item in the news: ANGRY HUSBAND SHOOTS WIFE! Where? Manhattan family court. As wife sits on bench in hall outside of courtroom, the husband writes a note and hands it to her. Wife tears it up. (Could they have been tenants here? Are the holes all that's left of marital target practise?) BANG, BANG, BANG! BANG, BANG, BANG! Goodbye—exit life! The holes are too small to be bullet holes; more likely they were left there by small nails hammered in to hold pictures. (But why so

10

many? So small? So close together?) Why are these perforations grouped together as if aimed at the heart of a (five-feet-eleven-inches) male with his back pressed to the crumbling plasterboard

**NOTE FOUND IN WASTEPAPER BASKET
AT PREVIOUS ADDRESS**

I love you. Come back to me or you'll be sorry.

I SHOULD HAVE SHOT JOSEF

Instead I chose to leave him, endangering myself. Think of how many lives could have been saved if the wife had moved out. Unfortunately this is not always possible. Unfortunately there are times one can't even move from room to room...or get out of bed to toast a muffin. This is the paralysing effect of one's husband going rat-a-tat-tat on one's skull. Apathy has always been thought of by the victim as a safe haven: the place where one can be alone. Wrongo! It is used as evidence against the wife: She Who Does Not Attend To Her Wifely Duties and deserves to be beaten.

WIFE: There's one thing I'll never understand—why I always obey you. Can you explain that to me?

HUSBAND: No...

WIFE: I'm tired of our fights, very tired.

Q: Was Josef violent? Verbally abusive? Your departure seems to have been abrupt.

A: No single disturbing event precipitated my departure; however, (at first barely noticeable) there was an insidious, increasing dullness; a gnawing dissatisfaction with life—also, the disappearance of *The Times* which I had arranged to have delivered daily to my home—and my disinclination to clip vegetarian recipes from Wednesday's Home Section.

My marriage had been *un*like any one of a number of marriages exposed on daytime talk shows.

Topic: **ABUSED WIVES**

11

One of them speaking, "He put his gun into my vagina, took it out and sucked on it, then he said, 'This is what love is all about.'

Josef was nice enough. Too nice. Always quiet and considerate. (Should I count those sudden, unexplained rages that came and went like summer squalls?) Hardly knew he was around. At times he'd stay out late. I could care less. Didn't ask questions. When he came home early, I'd pour him a drink. He liked Dewars Black Label. Expensivo. His mother (Marie) told me that he had had a scientific bent when he was young. Liked to dissect frogs, other dead animals: whatever he'd find lying in the road or behind his house in the woods. He'd wanted to be a doctor, white coat and all. I think he liked the look of it more than the application. Didn't have it in him to study all those years. To devote himself to it.

"Shadow crossed his path," his mother had confided, "it was then that he gave up on himself."

What shadow was she talking about?

Josef was at loose ends, taking odd jobs here and there until she lent him the money to open a pet store; but he couldn't manage that either. As previously noted: he was too kind (nice): he'd overfeed the mice till they dirtied their cages, then he'd cuss them out (as if they were to blame) because he had to clean up after them. Remorseful, he'd try to do better, give the tiny creatures hardly enough to eat; surprised him when they died of starvation!

Grown up as he was, Josef still enjoyed playing doctor. Would put on his soiled white coat, take scalpel in hand, and slice away as if pulling a violin bow across its strings. Oh, he was good at it, with those flawlessly executed movements; first he'd detach a leaf-thin section of flesh, then he'd cut an even thinner slice—till layer by layer the specimen was readied for microscopic scrutiny.

If he had played doctor the usual way, pretending to be a curious five year old—listening to my heart (his ear against my breast), or asking me to take my clothes off for a more thorough examination, I could have worked up some enthusiasm—but his absorption in the laboratory method of investigation left me cold. (However not cold enough for him.) "You want me to play dead, don't you!" I'd accuse. "Ha, ha, ha," he'd reply, "Ache head. Bad face. Bad bed." What shadow crossed his path, to make him give up on himself? Though all was quiet in that improvised back-of-shop laboratory, Josef would incline his head, listening to his thoughts: alert among the scales, calipers, and slides; unaware that I was there, waiting for him to come to supper.

INTENSITY FRIGHTENS ME

The more I was with him the less I wanted to be with him. He made love in a rush, throwing me to the bed, his heart beating fast—over and done with. What remained was the odor of cereal and dry milk powder—mouse food. Never a sophisticated male cologne. Never a whiff of imported English soap. Like sleeping with a rodent.

Q: It takes money to make a clean escape. Do you have enough to live on?

A: Some. Sold a video installation to a German collector. He said it looked nasty.

Q: Nasty?

A: Sexual...sadistic...you know—zippered mouths, helmets, whips, boots: my bad girl, bad boy phase. Punishment meted out for mysterious infringements. Psychic shit. The Germans go for that sort of thing. The Japanese like color, and balloons; something ephemeral, playful, noisy: rice paper wrapped jellies that melt in your mouth, ritual tea, stunted trees (stunted lady feet once upon a time), lanterns, computer Judo, pagodas, wind chimes, mountain climbs, hot tub family dips, bar girls and alcohol. Nice apology we got concerning Pearl Harbor: their secretaries couldn't type WE DECLARE WAR ON AMERICA! fast enough. (So sorry! Surprise attack unintentional.) Blame it on the office help. But they buy lots of art.

Q: From you?

A: Once upon a time.

Q: How do you feel about letting your work go?

A: It must be seen. If I had no chance of showing the work I wouldn't do it. I'd do something else.

Economy hadn't been the most important thing for me to consider when I left Josef. (What shadow crossed his path causing him to give up on himself?) I was in a hurry and looking for something immediately available. The room I first took was big enough for me, with private bath and phone. The phone was an absolute necessity, otherwise I would have been forced to make my calls from a phone booth on the corner. The floor was unpainted and splintery so I bought a cheap rug at the Floor Coverings store next door. Hadn't particularly liked the pattern: large black and blue flowers stenciled onto a neutral ground with a dull tan rectangle at its center; an absolutely unappealing utilitarian thing.

I hadn't lived there a month before my building burned down. The arsonist, it was thought, had made a mistake; his intended target had been the Floor Coverings store. For a while the store's owner had been the prime suspect—it was rumored that he was in debt. "LOST OUR LEASE! EVERYTHING MUST GO!" had certainly been an indication that things had gone from bad to worse. Perhaps the man, out of money and other solutions, had come to the conclusion that having his property set ablaze, then collecting the insurance would solve his financial woes.

During the initial investigation, a psychiatrist submitted that an arsonist's compulsion to set fires had a sexual motivation; (We're havin' a heat wave/a tropical heat wave/the temperature's risin'/ it aint so surprisin'...) and that arson, being a perfect joining of innate desire and the opportunity to make a buck, could become a virtual bonanza for the sexually distressed individual.

Q: Were you able to recover any of your work?

A: At the time most of my work was in storage.

Q: How did you feel?
A: Cursed. Frightened. Didn't know where to turn.
Q: And then?
A: I took refuge in "creative thinking." I thought, wouldn't a video cassette SHOWING a fire SATISFY an arsonist just as well as THE REAL THING, especially if the visuals were augmented by burning a few sheets of paper in the kitchen sink? Call it "The Olfactory Trigger Theory." All safe and under control. No harm done.

ARTISTS ARE CRAZY UNTIL PROVEN SANE
Too true.

LIFE CALLED INTO BEING FOR VIDEO PRESENTATION IS SOMETIMES ART

Using film, I discovered that whatever one sees or does can be made smaller and conveniently portable, or that if one is so inclined, the work can be enlarged to monumental proportions making it less portable but more visible (especially close-ups of, say, an eye being slit with a razor). It is a marvelous thing to see how the meaning of ones work changes with its size (size is the emphasis, the exclamation point). Size can crowd you out, or let you in. Remember that when you buy your ticket.

STOP ACTION

Stop-action particularly interests me—removing one image as if it were a talisman—keeping it for a reason not yet known/ for a scene not yet conceived. It's a kind of illegal appropriation: I rent films, find images I like, take them out.
These images are my found objects (*objets-trouvee*—as the French say). Editing film is the Splice of Life: unlikely juxtapositions made meaningful. And wouldn't I love to stop-action my life here and there. "Hey wait! Let's do it over again. Eliminate the negative, accentuate the positive!"

BARE INTERIOR—GREY LIGHT

"It's partially furnished," the landlord says, "just right for an artist like you; someone who can add the personal touch, be creative. A bargain in today's market; you don't take it, it'll go in a minute. Guaranteed."

AN ARTIST LIKE ME?

"It's a basement," I protest, "It's chilly..." allowing a tiny shiver, "and dark too."

"Yeah, sure, it's a basement. But it has a view. Two views in fact. A left view and a right view."

He indicates two windows high up on one wall with the curtains drawn.

"Late afternoon the sun shines its last right through those windows," he says, "It's glorious. Totally unexpected after the gray of morning. This place is full of delightful surprises. For instance, there's an eat-in kitchen back there, not one a them kitchenette numbers, take a look... and I've installed a fully tiled bathroom with shower. The water pressure's great (he demonstrates); watch out! Water's hot enough to boil eggs. Being in the basement is a plus, especially in the summertime. My own mother lived in a basement for almost sixty years. Never complained. You'll be as safe and comfortable here as you would be in an Egyptian tomb."

THIS UNDERGROUND MANSION OF DEATH

"I'll think it over," I say.
"Think fast."
"How fast?"
"Twenty-four hours?"
"I'd like to stay here awhile by myself, get the feel of the place."
"Stay as long as you like (Mr.Generous). Remember to

close the door when you leave."...pausing: "The homeless."
"The homeless?"
"Try to get in. Twist every doorknob up and down the block, just in case a door's unlocked. They're watchin' every minute. Piss on walls. Into corners. The stench of piss is fair warning...the end is at hand."
"You talking about...Armageddon? If you are, I can't take this apartment. I'm not ready to die."
"Good, then there should be no obstacle to signing a lease. One or two years? Your choice. You'll live at least that long. Wouldn't want to break the lease."
"I can live with that."
"Make yourself at home. You have any questions jot them down. Need a measuring tape? Always carry one with me."
"Thanks." I take it. It's new. Cloth. Not made of metal (not the kind with sharp edges that pulls out and snaps back, able to slice a finger). It's soft: winding tightly around itself, then uncoiling in my hand.
"There's a small ladder in the kitchen. You'll see. Last tenant left some stuff. Keep anything you want. Nobody's coming back for it; certainly not old Hamm; guy was on his last legs when the ambulance came and got' im. Believe me, he was more than ready to go: blind, weak capillaries, crippled, always in pain. This Clov guy he was livin' with flew the coop, left him to fend for himself. Yelling and cursing. Sturming and dranging, that's the way they lived. Glad they're gone. Made up my mind never to rent to men again: they don't take care of things, don't keep the property in tip-top shape, always dropping something down the drain: toothpaste top, broken razorblade, school ring—I can't afford to call the plumber in every damn day!"
"I'm the best tenant you'll ever have, Mr. Baltimore."
"Stan, call me Stan," he extends his hand. I pretend not to notice. We walk to the door.
At the door I flash a warm smile at Stan, the kind of smile Mata Hari might have used to get her way. I'm softening him

17

up for the kill: a reduction in the rent and two room-darkener window shades.

I close the door after him. Lock it. This is not a plot device in a thriller where one forgets to lock the door, allowing a murderer to enter. In the bathroom (No bath, a shower stall) there's still some paper on the roll: rough, cheap, the kind they feature in super-market sales; loss-leaders same as tomato soup, salami, paper towels, laundry detergent. The toilet flushes well enough, though the water's a little rusty. I pry a sliver of soap from the edge of the sink to wash my hands with: there's a large squashed roach pressed into it. A bottle of outdated prescription pills: Percodan is the only thing left in the medicine cabinet along with some rusty razor blades and a discount coupon for new ones.

In the kitchen, in a cabinet below the sink, I find a child's toy: a silky black dog with three legs. (He's a kind of Pomeranian: pug nose, small dark holes where his eyes had been, hidden behind a cataract of hair.) Something Josef might have experimented with when he was a child, before he discovered living creatures. There is some sandy/sawdusty filling leaking out. The work of mice I surmise. Noting that, I decide to buy a package of brillo (the soapless kind) to stuff into holes under the sink, around the steam pipes, and into suspicious spaces in the closets. Experience has taught me that rodents can cleverly avoid the traps set for them, but cannot bite through shredded metal, though some have tried.

Using my measuring tape, I find that the kitchen measures ten feet by ten feet; the ceiling (measured by eye) appears to be approximately ten feet high. Nice dimensions, nice proportions: a box of a kitchen. (As a child I'd hide in boxes. Was never afraid of the dark. Time stops in the dark, and the bad people can't find you.) I like to sit in kitchens. This kitchen will be a very inviting place when furnished...small round table, a few chairs, potted plant (preferably flowering cactus...hardly needs looking after...pink bloom or yellow...never fades, never falls...a delight forever in the absence of other delights) also a burnt-sienna glazed bowl for fruit, and this forgotten old alarm clock in the shape of a tea kettle.

Q: The alarm, is it working? (Setting the alarm. Releasing it).

A: Ringing fit to wake the dead. (It works.)

Opening the largest closet, between the entryway and the living room, I see an old wooden wheelchair; most probably the one that Mr. Hamm tooled around in. It has no cushion, needs a coat of paint and a set of rubber runners for its wheels. I wonder, would it be worth the expense to fix it? But what do I need a wheelchair for? A wheelchair that might take up too much room, or creak mysteriously at night frightening me.

A chair wants to be occupied: to serve its purpose. When left alone, a chair, like a dog might make unhappy sounds that only the neighbors hear. And then, through no fault of my own I'd be accused of cruelty. I'll have to figure it out. But not now.

I roll it to the center of the living room, where once I have positioned it (stopped it from rolling by wedging an old paperback book beneath one wheel) it presides stanchly over the empty room. Good enough. I'm tired. I sit in it, hard as the seat is... and as I sit there, I notice a strange smell.

My nose leads me to the kitchen again, where I find nothing—no gassy bags of forgotten peelings turned to mulch, no dead rodent partially liquified in defrosting pan beneath the fridge, no forgotten turd sending a final message from its hoary hiding place. Then what is it? My sense of smell is one of the best senses I have, having failed me only once, after I had been ill with a virus...at that time I couldn't smell grass after a rain, or fresh baked bread...I hadn't even been able to smell myself! My appetite had remained intact, but the actual relish of eating (and of sex), had been momentarily diminished.

I've had enough. The origin of stench will have to be

searched out another time.

I like the place well enough. The living room, (which has four electric outlets, two at the baseboards of each wall, to plug in computers and video equipment) will suit me fine as a studio...I can stop up the holes I noticed in the wall with plaster, or as a stop-gap measure hang a large poster of Jane Avril over them.

Q: Regarding the previous tenants? Do you think their names are pseudonymous?—chosen to explain their relationship to one another and possibly to the world? Hamm! Clov!

A: Oh. Yes I do. Actually there are two kinds of ham...one is food: smoked or fresh pig flesh. The other ham describes an overinflated actor much taken with himself. Mr. Hamm's name encompasses both of these hams. As for Clov—A clove is a sharp little tack of a spice often used to flavor ham. It is done this way: one takes a knife and scores the ham, dividing its fatty surface into diamonds—into each of these divisions a clov is inserted, to be left there while the ham bakes. If the pig were alive it would be a painful procedure—one that Josef would approve of—however, cloves are an excellent spice with which to flavor a ham—to compliment its appetizing aroma.

Q: So this Mr. Hamm and his companion Clov complimented one another.

A: Except when Hamm behaved in a highly theatrical manner; at that time he may have been trying for laughs to cheer himself up—or, as a committee of one, had elected himself to represent those of us who are willing to make fools of ourselves for small reward: e.g. the spontaneous, salutory kudo. Up to a point, misery can use a good laugh; beyond that point nothing helps. Therefore it seems to me, judging from their names and from what they left behind, that these former tenants lived lives of entrenched misery relieved only by bits of ascerbic wit (jokes at their own expense).

QUOTE

"Nothing is funnier than unhappiness. Yes, yes, it's the most comical thing in the world." (Sam Beckett)
Q: Will you get a pet to keep you company?
A: Not even a real dog!
Q: What if Josef finds you here?
A: I'll tell him I've had enough.
Q: Yes!...Of what?
A: Of this...this...thing.

RENTAL UPDATE

Good news! I'm here officially for one year at a reduced rent; Mr. Baltimore has agreed to provide window shades. Small triumphs. My warm smile convinced him that I'd be an ideal tenant. Perhaps he was dreaming of an invitation to tea, where after the scones and clotted cream were consumed, we'd party. Fat chance! The lease is signed, sealed, delivered, and secure within a locked metal box that I have prudently stashed on a closet shelf.

UNEXPECTED VISIT

"I really like you," Mr. Stan Baltimore says, "feel as if I already know you. You feel that way about me?" (Hopefully.)
"No."
"You have beautiful legs. I'd like to see them in stockings, garterbelt, and high heels. You ever dress up in things like that?" (Hopefully.)
"No."
"Guess I'll go now." (Ruefully.)
"Okay."

ORIENTATION

My equipment is plugged in, ready to go. The empty

tapes haven't been unboxed yet, but old tapes, treated as if they were archival treasures by me, rest in a specially built slotted crate.

It's getting dark. I've been putting things away for hours. I miss the light. I want to see what is out there. I pull the ladder to just below the window on the right. Lift the curtain. I hear footsteps before I see the feet of people passing by. A gum wrapper drops to the sidewalk: it is green. Someone spits a shiny globule of phlegm: it is translucent and wobbles.

Someone retrieves a cigarette stub that is all filter. A man in torn jeans relieves himself against the side of the building. Some of the urine courses down my window making Pollock drawings in the dust. I take still photos of the window. Use up an entire roll of film. Want to save the window just as it is; use the stills for an essay on urine. Urine is so useful: it shimmers, it changes color, it sterilizes open wounds, it carries impurities from the body, and in some circles is considered a turn-on...though for degradation/elation some of my friends, Kathy BienSur for one, prefer body piercing. She has two nose rings. And one ring through the nipple of her left breast. Gives me the shivers. I'm so uncool. So what.

I BROADEN MY HORIZONS

I've bought into the Art Internet and am caught in an ever expanding computer confab: global developments, electronic chat, and other hellish data just a hook up away. My doppelganger who goes by the pseudonym of Nana, travels the same information highway, where we discuss wide range art with each other. This is really having your cake and eating it too: I'm alone in my room yet simultaneously abroad in the world. Ideal situation, no?

artfab@mama.ed

Hi, it's Nana. This gallery show: embalmed schools of fish in museum cases. Is it a comment on natural history, or a new version of Portuguese salted cod?

IT IS THE JOB OF THE CURATOR TO CATEGORIZE, TO MAKE CONNECTIONS. WE ARE ALL PART OF A SYSTEM. WE CAN BE *COD*-IFIED, PUT INTO SOME KIND OF ORDER, THOUGH MOST OF US WILL NOT BE PUT ON DISPLAY AFTER DEATH— LAID SHOULDER TO SHOULDER IN SIZE PLACES—OR MADE TO RECLINE ON BANKED GRANITE BEDS INSCRIBED WITH OUR NAMES AND ACCOMPLISH-MENTS. FOR EXAMPLE.

RIP

HERE LIES MARAINI, JULIA
SHE'S REALLY DEAD
DON'T LET HER FOOLYA
SHAMAN OF THE SELF IN ART
SAY GOODBYE TO HEAD AND HEART
OF JULIA. AMEN.

Hey Julia, what's the connection between shame and shaman? Is there any? Think about it. Catch you later.

2

Mr. J.G.O., the president of a steel factory in Brazil, will be here any minute: met him in the lobby of the Walter Reade Theater (near Juilliard) after a showing of a movie about Schubert. He picked me up: "What do you think of the movie?" He asked, "Did you like it?"

DIALOGUE

HE: Did you like the movie?

ME: Yes. Especially the way Schubert's hair fell out and the way the lesions on his hands looked like tiny craters. The hospital he was in appeared to be a mad house. No cure for Syphillis then: so when it went into remission they thought it was gone for good. What'd you think of the movie?

HE: I liked it too. However I prefer the old version of Schubert, the romantic one. Poor Schubert. He was, unfortunately, a repressed man who could not dance. His sense of rhythm never reached his feet. It stayed in his head. It animated his fingers. It pounded in his chest. But it ignored his feet.

ME: True, he didn't know the latest dance steps, but he did get to go to a lot of parties and play the piano. Gee I hated it when the rains came and rained on all that food: so many beautiful cakes ruined. Don't you hate movies that have such great food but nobody eats it? I mean, I know that the beggar who followed Schubert to the party stuffed his mouth, but nobody else did. I could have jumped right into the movie to eat those cakes.

HE: Would you like to have some cake and coffee with me?

ME: Some other time. Gotta run.

Rosalyn Drexler

HE: Well here's my card. Please call me. I'd love to continue this discussion with you...however I'm returning to Brazil later this month, so don't wait too long to call me.

I call him the very next day.

PREPARING FOR HIS VISIT—A SMELL!

That awful odor is still here. Probably behind the wall. I haven't mentioned it to the landlord (Mr. Stan Baltimore); maybe I should—this is his property; he knows where the bodies are buried (just a figure of speech I hope).

The doorbell rings. My guest is here.

VIDEO INTERVIEW WITH MR. J.G.O.

Q: Tell me what you do.
A: I am president of Companhia Diderurgia National, Rio de Janeiro, Brazil. For lunch I had veal with sauce, spinach, and potato washed down with a good Valpolicello. After which the flaming marshmallow ice-cream cake was served. I thought of you.
Q: Thank you.
A: I wanted to bring you a piece, but it would have melted in my pocket.
Q: I appreciate the thought. So...tell me about your life in Brazil.
A: I work hard all day. Come home and go to sleep. My wife would like a more active social life. Too bad. I can't change. On the weekends I like to take care of my cows. I have a farm. This is what I really like to do. It relaxes me. I married late in life, when I was already in my forties. I have no children of my own, but my wife has a son who is now married. My daughter-in-law...
He hesitates, shifting in the wheelchair. His legs are too long to rest easily on the footrest—they stretch out in front of

25

him, heels to the floor, knees locked.

Q: Your daughter-in-law?

A: She cares about me, asks where I'm going, how I feel, when I'm coming back...My wife cares for me too...However the problem is that I sometimes regard my daughter-in-law as a...woman. This is as far as it will go. A strong attraction. I dare not act on my desire, buy it is there.

Q: Are you attracted to me?

A: You are a beautiful woman.

Q: As beautiful as one of your cows?

His eyes close, his face softens, as he enters a world of outrageous amorous exploit; a world he now describes to me in the most vulgar terms: "One day in the cow barn...alone...the hired help is out eating...I notice that one of the cows is in heat...She's got a cunt just like my wife...I take out my prick and shove it into her. But the cow doesn't stay put. I lift her tail up and this enables me to keep it in. I manage to screw her alright, and enjoy it more than with my wife. But, she shits all over me; my balls and trousers are covered with the stuff. That's why I never tried to screw her again. It is a more common occurrence than you realize."

Q: Every man has his speciality.

A: I've never confessed it to anyone.

Q: Why me?

A: Because you are a stranger.

Q: But I've just documented your confession...If the Whitney Museum chooses to show my videos, you'll be famous for fucking a cow.

A: Better that than being famous for owning a steel mill in Brazil.

Q: Why better?

A: In Brazil there is extreme poverty at one end, with great wealth at the other; someday, maybe soon, there will be a revolt. Our capability to produce steel is immense, but the market is dwindling.

On taking his leave: "I like the way it smells in here: like

26

a barn. Or is it my imagination?"
"You're not imagining it."
"Perhaps you should open a window?"
"Wouldn't help anyway."

A black Mercedes Benz waits for him. When he emerges from my basement his chauffeur jumps out, holds the car door open for him, and he gets in; chauffeur closes door, and off they go.

AN IDEA

For the installation I will paint a picture of a cow on a piece of metal. Seated in the wheelchair a naked man watching (on TV monitors) modern milking and pasteurization methods. The interview on a looped tape will repeat itself endlessly. Make of it what you will. I have.

A GRISLY DISCOVERY

Galvanized trash bins. Two of them side by side as if married. Twin receptacles of equal size in a hidden recess between the refrigerator and the stove. I am led there by a strong odor, possibly the origin of what I have been smelling throughout the apartment. I pull the first one out. It is heavy. With what? I start to remove the tightly fitted cover, first prying it up on one side, then continuing on, till little by little the entire cover loosens. At this point I am greeted by a sickly stink: an ancient olfactory offering of rotting flesh. I remove the cover. There is no flesh in the bin; perhaps at one time there had been, but now I find only bones resting upon a thin floor of sand. I withdraw in horror.

RECYCLING

Josef has a skull that he uses as an ashtray. It is the skull of an old man. He said it was his father's skull.

In rebuttal, Josef's mother (Marie) said to me, "Don't believe everything you hear."

Why would Josef have lied to me? If relatives carry the ashes of loved ones home from the crematory in ordinary coffee cans (no disrespect intended) why not take the skull too? A cranium without its brain can still be a useful thing: a place to store rolled up socks for instance...even the humerus (formerly part of the arm) can continue to perform as a drum beater, or soup stirrer...the ribs (after sterilization and bleaching) provide an excellent carving substance, being as hard as ivory or whalebone: native New Yorkers have been known to use this superior material in order to achieve an incomparable effect: carvings of model airplanes, napkin rings, and miniature hypodermic needles.

Gathering courage I peek into the trash bin again: force myself to observe the skull. It reminds me of a skull made of synthetic material that I saw displayed in the window of a souvenir shop. The skull found in my trash bin is also a souvenir, though hardly a sentimental one.

WHAT I DO WITH MY DISCOVERY

I film the trash bins and their contents: (each houses its own skeleton and skull). Make myself a cup of Earl Grey tea.

Reflect upon my next move. I can either call 911, or the landlord. Hamm and Clov were the last tenants. However this place has been unoccupied for over a year. How long have the skeletons been here?

This is the kind of place Josef would find suitable for his unholy pursuits: a basement burial ground; sound controlled (no cries can be heard), lots of water to wash bloody hands, and a secure mailbox to receive his government checks.

ONE DAY JOSEF WILL KILL ME

He will, nice as he is. Among other things he is insanely jealous of me. Refused to let me have my teeth capped for fear

28

I'd smile at strangers, a thing I would never do.

"A smiling woman is an unfaithful woman," he'd say.

Can you imagine my feeling sorry for him? I do. I always manage to find excuses for his odd behavior. What shadow passed over him, to make him give up on himself? Fuck him anyway, when I get the money I'm gonna fix my teeth, I haven't given up on myself. I call Juan Ferra, holding back the big news: skeletons found in my closet! I let him tell me his news first: he's won the 1993 Skowhegan School of Painting and Sculpture medal for sculpture.

"I'm self taught," he confides, "art schools are full of shit. Imagine them giving me an award! Bill DeKooning never even got a Guggenheim. How do they decide these things?"

"So, did you make a speech?"

"I thanked them for the honor, got drunk, and put the make on Lucy the Lip who was there as a presenter. She gave me the brush. Think she's gay?"

"Isn't everyone? So who won for video/installation?"

"How the fuck do I know."

"You always know."

"Okay. Bill Viola. Jealous?"

"Why should I be jealous?"

"You want to win."

"I'm good. I should win."

"So tell me how you've been? Heard about you and Josef. Any chance for me now?"

"Sure; I've had the hots for you ever since we met...Hey, you won't believe this...but this place I moved into...I was looking around...there were these two trash bins in the kitchen...guess what was in 'em!"

"Money? Jewels?...Drugs?"

"Bones! Human bones. Two complete skeletons!"

"What a find! (excited) You must give one to me! I need it for my next piece: SKELETON ON BURNED MATTRESS WITH HALF FULL TUBE OF KY JELLY, A PACKAGE OF CONDOMS, AND A MICKEY MOUSE WATCH. It's for the AIDS benefit at White Columns. The new location."

"I was about to call the police...or the landlord. Boy I'm not keen on having people tramp all over the place—You're in that show? Why didn't they ask me?"
"I agree. It'd be a bitch!—Didn't know you wanted to be in it."
"Forget it.—Yeah, I'd have to move again."
"Right; so live with your secret."
"Sure."
"You free this Saturday? I'm planning a party. People you should meet: artists, collectors, others...rounded up the usual suspects."
"I'd love to come...if I'm still alive."
"Why shouldn't you be?"
"Josef...he's nuts."
"Wouldn't hurt a flea. I do think he should take care of his habit though."
"Habit? Josef doesn't use."
"Snapple. He drinks far too much of it. Saw him downing it by the quart at Dean & De Lucas. Must have adult onset Diabetes...Saturday then?"
"What time?"
"Any time after nine dear, and bring your appetite; Frank's doing a sumptuous spread: gonna be finger lickin' good."

INTERVIEWING SKELETONS—YES!

I drop my idea about interviewing only men for the next year. I am eager to interview women again (Why?) (Why not?)...and of course will closely question the skeletons who should not be judged by gender alone. To be fair, I intend to measure their pelvic basins, consult my Gray's Anatomy for clues. Data is an important part of my art. Proof is needed for even the wildest archeological speculation; otherwise the critics will have you over a barrel (or in one lined with nails). However, I am really curious to hear what these skeletons have to say e.g. comparisons between their former fully fleshed selves and their empty clattering un-life in the present. They probably don't understand the concept of present/past/future since they "hang" outside of time: are just here doing nothing and wanting nothing. Will science find a way to recycle these armitures for entire body transplants? Am I climbing the wrong mountain for enlightenment?

To freshen the air (alter it's odor chemically) I put in a month's supply of Summer Rain air freshener. Down here it's imperative. However, I hope that there will be no bad effects from its use.

I buy a bright halogen lamp. This, in spite of reports that it is unhealthy to remain in the vicinity of a halogen lamp for too long. There is a store nearby that sells newspapers and magazines. How conveenient. This in itself can't hurt me, unless fate intervenes and I'm accidently dropped by a bullet meant for someone else. "Drive By Drug Vendetta" is not my favorite song, and I don't have no quarters to waste.

3

Josef appears to me in a dream. We are here watching my interview with the man from Brazil (on the VCR), eating unsalted popcorn from a green plastic bowl, having a good time, when suddenly Josef's body begins to glow. I watch in stunned horror as he is eaten alive—by my TV! Josef's body breaks apart into tiny particles before vanishing into a cloud of vapor. I explain to his mother (Marie) who materializes out of the wallpaper that Josef is a TV junkie who refuses to eat for fear of missing his favorite programs, all based on my latest video-interview series. "Yes," she says, "I know. I couldn't drag him away from the screen either." She begins screaming. The TV set is shaking on its stand. I can hear Josef's voice fading away as his cloud is sucked into the picture tube. (Ironically, Josef's father ((now deceased)) was a TV repairman by profession. He'd arrived in this country without any skills, saw an advertisement for a TV Repair Academy on the back of a package of matches, entered the Academy on a student loan, got his diploma, bought a set of tools...and voila, became a self-sufficient product of the American dream.) Josef can barely be heard. He tells me that he is finally where he wants to be, but that he will come out from time to time to visit me. A detective is having a hard time swallowing my story. He accuses me of having seen too many sci-fi horror films.

"I believe you're covering up a kidnapping, or a murder," he says to me. "Does your husband have any enemies that you know of? Or has he ever expressed a desire to leave you?"

I can't begin to enumerate the number of enemies Josef has, beginning with me.

I shake my head sadly, "As far as I know Josef has no enemies, so you can certainly rule out foul play."

A psychic, who looks a lot like my friend Kathy BienSur,

sits in the detective's lap; she confirms my amazing tale, "Josef is alive and well, dwelling within the airwaves of Julia Maraini's television set," she wails, "He is a being of ultra-high vibrational frequency who is able to dissolve his earthly shell into particles of energy which are now circulating within this set's picture tube."

"Happy at last," Josef's mother says, "A citizen of two worlds."

"It was the popcorn," I say, "he choked on it."

When Josef's father died, Josef was five years old. Very soon after, Marie (his mother), remarried. Josef was still five years old. Her second husband Dwayne tried to beat Josef to death when he was unable to get past the letter "H" in reciting the alphabet. No matter what Dwayne did, Josef wouldn't or couldn't learn the rest of the alphabet. His real daddy had only gotten him up to the letter "H". "I" would have been next no doubt if his daddy hadn't died on him. Somehow Josef got it into his little head that he had killed his daddy. No way he was going to learn the rest of that alphabet till his daddy came back and taught it to him himself.

"Dwayne thought Josef was holding out on him," Marie told me, "so he beat him with his hands, a belt, and a stick. I was sick in bed when I heard Dwayne yelling at the kid, 'Do it again!' Then he began beating the boy. He punched him several times, hit him with a belt, then went outside and got a big stick, and struck him several more times. I didn't know he was beating Josef until the child ran into my room and collapsed."

This is the first shadow that passed over Josef, making him give up on himself: afterwards he was unable to understand words containing letters of the alphabet above "H". Comfortable with bad, face, he, egg, be, da, age, gag, and so forth, such pivotal words as sex, love, hate, male, female, death, and the all important "I" remained entirely outside his comprehension, as did the words marriage and ma.

4

BACK TO WORK

**INTERVIEW WITH TWO SKELETONS
OF INDETERMINATE GENDER**

> Setting: a basement
> living room in romantic
> half-light. Two
> galvanized trash cans
> beside each other.
> Music: Video-artist sings
> ALL OF ME.
> As song ends one skull
> appears above rim of
> trash bin.

SKELETON 1
Love that melody. Can you see me?
I can't see you.

Q: Were you asleep?

> Roach appears. Crawls.

SKELETON 1 (cont'd)
Oh no. Waiting.

Q: Oh yes.

> Roach goes up trash bin,
> feelers quivering.

SKELETON 1 (cont'd)
Time for harmonicas?

Q: Always time for harmonicas.
                                    Roach reaches rim of trash
                                    bin. Hangs there.

        SKELETON 1 (cont'd)
        She disagrees.
        (Indicates other trash bin)

                            Skull of skeleton 2 appears
                            above rim of
                            second trash bin.

        SKELETON 2
        (SKELETON sees roach)
        Look, a living creature—kill it.
                (pauses)
        I don't disagree. If one has time, there's time for
        harmonicas. Blind old men play harmonica. They
        make time for it.

Q: I've squashed it.

        SKELETON 1
        Thank you.
                (To skeleton 2)
        Then how about a kiss?

        SKELETON 2
        I would if I could but I can't.
        Who took my tasty red wax lips?

        SKELETON 1
        Hamm chewed 'em up.

Q: Hamm? The famous literary invalid? The hypochondriacal sadist?

SKELETON 1 (cont'd)
Yes, that's the one. Hamm's our only son. He said our social security check would help him pay the rent, so he brought us here. We did eat so little.

SKELETON 2
A few crackers, soup, sometimes raspberry jello. Made me feel faint.

SKELETON 1
Starved us to death. Used the same teabag half a dozen times at least. Weak tea for weak people is cruel: strong tea is a great treat. He was very selfish. Wanted everything for himself and Clov.

SKELETON 2
Bought himself a slave, that's what.

SKELETON 1
What?

SKELETON 2
Got old fast.

SKELETON 1
Ah yes, all is past.

SKELETON 2
The past! (elegiac) Six tiny larks, songbirds, cooked and charred whole: heads, eyes, and beaks intact— wings intact—tiny bony legs.

SKELETON 1
Arranged around a mound of polenta. What a

fragrant funeral pyre.

SKELETON 2
A bird that size is almost all liver. Tastes like paté.

SKELETON 1
One has to have an educated palate to eat larks.

SKELETON 2
And a healthy bank account.
Q: I was told that you were pursued by terrorists. Is that true?

SKELETON 1
Are you speaking of the time our mailbox exploded? Just a bit of plastique put there by Clov.

SKELETON 2
A practical joke.

SKELETON 1
Almost killed us.

Q: Why? Did he explain?

SKELETON 1 (cont'd)
Till he was blue in the face.

SKELETON 2
Didn't get very far with me.

SKELETON 1
Could have made a federal case out of it.

SKELETON 2
Hamm stopped you just in the nick of time.

SKELETON 1
Otherwise where would we have been?

SKELETON 2
Put away.

Q: Terrorism does work; after all where are you now?

SKELETON 1
Implying what?

Q: That you've been put away for good.

SKELETON 1 (cont'd)
Don't mistake the natural course of events with...damp! Where's my sand?

SKELETON 2
At the seashore.

SKELETON 1
Don't remind me. You challenged the boy. He was afraid of the ocean. You shouted. He entered the waves and almost drowned. Why didn't you cease and desist?

SKELETON 2
The color came back into his little cheeks.

SKELETON 1
You lost patience. You controlled us by losing patience.

SKELETON 2
Don't cry. Please don't cry. Are you crying?

SKELETON 1
We are ended up. Finished.
Q: Would you like to go back in?

SKELETON 1 (cont'd)
You must understand that we love each other in
spite of hating one another. (Alarmed) What's
happened to our stuffing? Our skin? There's nothing left to pinch. (Metacarpus to cranium) No fever
in the flesh. No shivers.

Q: But you shake, rattle and role. (a miserable attempt at
humor)

SKELETON 2
Only when hung in the wind like a chime.

SKELETON 1
If we had brought Hamm up properly, he might
have been somebody. His nosebleeds...Hard hand
to boy's nose. One of those sudden squalls of
anger.

SKELETON 2
Who's sorry now?

SKELETON 1
No way to make amends.

SKELETON 2
Such a sensitive child: nearsighted, nervous,
bronchitic, and asthmatic, and he loved the wrong
things—theater, for one.

SKELETON 1
He had a distaste for Germans and loathed dogs.

SKELETON 2
He loved dogs.
SKELETON 1
Not unfinished dogs.

SKELETON 2
Unfinished?

SKELETON 1
The sex. I told him, "The sex goes on at the end.
After the sex we put on his ribbon!"

SKELETON 2
Ah yes, his toy dog. Bought it at Salvation Army.
An incomplete mutt inordinately loved by our
son.

SKELETON 1
Lucky dog!

Q: I found this poem tucked into a crack in the wall. Tell me
if you can, whether it was your son Hamm who wrote it.

(reading)
THERE WAS A QUEER MAN KNOWN AS LILLIAN
WHO PAINTED HIS CHEEKS WITH VERMILLION
WHEN THEY SAID, "YOU'RE A MALE!" AT FAK-
ING YOU FAIL,
HE MADE HIS REPLY POST COTILLION.

As I interpret it—this Lillian who was a transvestite was not
very good at disguising his gender, and, since dancing was his
favorite pastime before his accident, he wouldn't let anything
interfere with it. Being a polite person however, he answered
his detractor after the dance (POST COTILLION).

40

SKELETON 2
Hamm did dabble in verse. I remember the very
incident. His answer came in the form of a right to
the jaw, knocking his tormentor Clov to the ground.

SKELETON 1
Lillian was Hamm and Hamm was Lillian.

SKELETON 2
It is a love poem: insult and retribution.

SKELETON 1
I'm ready to go back in...and you love?

SKELETON 2
Me too.

As I push the skeletons (carefully) back down into their
cylindrical lairs, someone sighs.

ANCIENT WISDOM

SHE: "Love makes the world go 'round."
HE: "So does a punch in the jaw."

5

KATHY CALLS

Kathy BienSur is on the phone. She says she is wearing her red-red lipstick and has brushed her black-black hair for me. She likes to feel seductive, even on the phone.

"Something catastrophic is about to happen," she intones, "call Marie."

"Is she in danger?"

"Someone close to her is."

"What if she wants to know why I've called."

"She won't."

"She'll trace the phone call and give my number to Josef!"

"She won't."

"Is that all you can tell me?"

"I was wondering whether you'd consider lending your name to a project I'm involved in called The Abortion Project.... We're covering an entire wall with the signatures of famous and near famous women who've had abortions. It's gonna be great."

"Does spontaneous abortion count?"

"Explain."

"I was visiting Stratford Connecticut for the Shakespeare Festival, eating lunch, when all of a sudden I didn't feel so good, so I went to the toilet, and this transparent golf ball thing came out of me. Nothing was in it. It was really magical. And then I bled. I bled all the way through the play. And I bled when I got home. After that I wasn't pregnant any more. So do I qualify for your project?"

"Hey I gotta go. Remember to call Marie, okay?"

"You coming to Juan's party?"

"Saturday?"

"Yeah. I'd like to tell you what I'm doing...it's fabulous...."
"Later babe—at the party." (Line goes dead)

artfab@mama.ed

Hi. I've had these real bad menstrual cramps. My womb
is tipped. Doctor says if I have a child the pain will go away. I'd
kill myself if I got pregnant. What should I do?
TRANSLATE YOUR PAIN: MAKE ART NOT BABIES.
SAW A SHOW OF MENSTRUAL BLOOD IN ANTIQUE
BOTTLES LABELED BY MONTH AND YEAR. 1993 WAS A
GOOD YEAR FOR MENSES-SEC. RICH BOUQUET.
SMOOTH. DEEP COLOR. THE SANG(RIA) OF CHOICE
AMONG WINE CONNOISSEURS. WHETHER YOU PREFER
YOURS SANG FROID, OR CHAUD IT'S BOUND TO MAKE
YOU THE MOST TALKED ABOUT HOST IN TOWN. HEY,
TRY DEMEROL FOR THE PAIN AND STAY IN BED.

AT JUAN'S PARTY

"I was so worried about you," Juan says.
"Why?"
"You got me worried. Don't you remember?"
"No."
"About Josef."
"Oh...I'm okay today. He don't worry me today."
"Thanks for keeping me informed! (Head turning in
direction of woman) See that gorgeous lady? She wants to
meet you." (Takes deep breath. Hesitates.)
"Well, who the fuck is she already?"
"A founding sister of Brit feminism, here to promote her
first novel. I took the liberty of suggesting that you might want
to interview her for American TV."
"You're such an evil, perverted, ungodly pain in the ass!"
"I know. I described your work to her as the purest
possible vision of the heart and soul filled with pathos and
humanity."

"Ugh! Everything I hate in a work of art. How could you?"

"Easy. I'm the devil, remember?"

"Now I really need some food and drink to sustain me. Where's that feast Frank cooked up?"

"Follow me."

The goodies are laid out on a trestle table in the studio, one end saved for the drinks: red and white wine, salt-free seltzer, other sodas. I put some vine leaves, chickpeas, rice and lamb on a plate. Fill my glass with red wine.

"Kathy's coming." Juan says, as if relaying bad news.

"I know."

Sitting on an overstuffed couch. Green velour. Gilded frame. Coffee table holding plates of cheese, fruit, and crackers. The Brit is nibbling on a cracker spread with pebbly crumbs of blue-veined cheese. She is ill at ease. Glancing around to find someone who might be interesting/important to talk to. Juan introduces us then disappears. I barely hear the woman's name. I don't think she remembers mine. She is slender, tall, with short dark hair and glittery blue eyes. I wonder if the glitter is drug induced or the result of a soothing application of Visine after her long plane trip. Ms. Brit looks fashionable without trying: dressed in sheer layers of skirt, blouse, jacket, scarf. The fabric, obeying the credo that "anything goes," mixes dots, flowers, and zigzag lines. Her mobile tongue (I can't help but notice it, since it seems such an intelligent appendage), herds bits of cheese into her mouth. Nevertheless some maverick crumbs manage to fall to the rug.

She shrugs her shoulders, "Hard to eat this without being a slob."

Juan's dog, a fully grown mongrel (obviously a complete dog with tumescent genitalia attached) patters over hoping for a handout. His pleading stare and drip-mouthed panting is hardly appealing. As he edges closer I aim a well placed kick to his left flank, sending him away.

"I like your scarf," I say, "the muted colors are quite unusual."

"It's yours," she says, winding it around my neck.

"Mine?" I'm embarrassed. It was only a conversational gambit. I don't like it that much.

"I bought a few in Milan, just in case...Looks pretty on you."

"Thanks. Real silk. Wow...You were in Milan?"

"Yes. (very animated) Did you know that the airport in Milan is called MALPENSA? Translated that means bad thought."

"Bad thought. What a name for an airport!"

"Luckily my plane didn't crash...I'm sorry, I didn't catch your name when Juan introduced us."

"Julia. Julia Maraini."

"Oh, you're Italian. You look Irish."

"My mother is Irish."

"What a combination: gift of gab, passionate attachments."

"And you're British, that's obvious."

"To the core. I'm Jane Birch, also known as Jane Bitch."

"You're boasting."

"I know. I'm actually a very nice person."

"Juan told me about your book..."

"Read page forty-five...my female protagonist gets fucked in the snow and doesn't feel cold till ten minutes later. You should try it."

"I like the sun."

"Well I do too: sitting on the beach watching those well tanned muscular men go by. Can't stand pale, weak men. Once I knocked the wind out of a bloke just because he didn't have a tan. Got in all the papers. They said I did it for the publicity. Bloody right!...You interested in doing a video of me? I can be terrifically outrageous or mournfully mousey within the space of half a second—it's that manic-depression thing—I'm either digging my own grave, or swinging crazily above a garden of forbidden epithets."

"I get personal."

"Of course."

45

"Sometimes I get too close for comfort."

"One thing leads to another." She sings the next line: "Too late to run for cover." Speaking: "I once fancied myself a singer."

"Where are you staying?"

"Nowhere and anywhere. My publisher's putting me up for the weekend, after that I don't know. Juan said he'd ask around."

On impulse I offer her my own place to crash. "You can stay with me, if you don't mind sleeping on the floor."

"I'll borrow a sleeping bag from Juan. Thank you. Thank you very much. You come to Cambridge, I'll return the favor."

I don't see myself in Cambridge any time soon. She'll have to return the favor some other way—lunch at the Tribeca Grill? She removes herself from me and heads toward Juan and Frank who're arguing as usual: their voices rise to an ear-splitting pitch. Mercifully, Ann interrupts, taking Juan aside. They then disappear into his studio. Frank sees me, waves me over.

"Chickens with their heads twisted off; makeshift altar; everything soaked in blood. Slaughter of chickens don't bother me. It's the number of missing children around the country." Frank shakes his head in disbelief.

"Santeria?" I ask.

"Not my religion," he replies. "Ask Juan, he's a believer."

"You been fighting again?"

"Accused me of using instant rice in the stuffed vine leaves. I swear I'd never do that."

"I believe you dear."

"Thanks Julia...Oh my God, there's that guy Juan insists is a genius."

The guy (hereupon to be known as The Guy) joins us: "You've just moved!" he says, "Juan tells me you need help with the decor...I can help you. Look at these designs (takes sketches from a black laminated-paper portfolio—imported from France—featured in the window of a Fifth Avenue art store—I had wanted to buy one—didn't) they're exclusively mine. You like something, we can make an arrangement satisfactory to both of us."

One of the sketches reminds me of the rug design I disliked so much (until it grew on me): black and blue flowers on a neutral tan background if I remember correctly; a really crappy rug. "You designed that?" My finger rests on the sketch.

"You like it?" He is already preening; ready to exact a price for his monotonous shit.

"I had a rug with flowers just like that," I admit, "but it burned in a fire. Wasn't sorry to see it go either."

He senses he is losing me as an admirer: "Lots of things look alike but aren't (petulantly). I haven't sold this design yet. It's exclusive. (reviving) I can put it on matched towels for you—you need curtains?"

"I don't have any money," I say. "Why don't you try some of Juan's collector friends."

"You don't have to pay me," he insists. "You're an important video artist—you can make me famous." I look at this worm with disdain; he wants me to document his dreary life, "Sorry, I'm booked for three years running."

He doesn't let me go—clutches at my sleeve. Does he really want me to expose him as somebody to avoid; is he determined to humiliate himself? The man gets his ideas from chintz couch throws, and artificial turf (his penchant for shiny green). I could vomit.

"I have information that concerns you," he declares importantly. "There is more to me than meets the eye. That fire in the carpet store—it was not set accidently by a man with a cigarette lighter. They have the wrong guy." His voice drifts off mysteriously. As he turns on his heel: "Juan has my phone number. Call me. You won't be sorry. I'm the one who started the rage for furniture as art: was commissioned to reupholster designer wheelchairs for the Modern, and I can make three-legged dogs dance without batteries." He rushes away, eager to pitch his wares to anyone willing to listen.

I turn to Frank who has not moved from the spot. "Who

told you about this Santeria thing: the missing kids? Was it on the evening news?"

"No." He pours a shot of Tequila for himself. "I found some chicken feathers and part of a child's shoe in one of Juan's burned mattresses."

"So what! I eat chicken, don't you? Someone has to kill them—as for the shoe, don't you remember when Payless had a sale and Juan bought all them kiddie shoes for an installation?"

"He's been very, very strange lately. Gets his chickens live(!) from some butch gal runs a poultry farm in New Jersey. And then there's all these melting candles! I can't stand the smell of tallow scented with bayberry, or sandalwood! I'm going out of my mind in this teahouse of the sacrificial faggot."

I am not about to interfere in a lover's quarrel. I've had too many of them myself. I ignore Frank's hysteria. He'll get over it. The man just doesn't understand Juan's work. After all he's the one who actually pissed into a Bob Gober urinal (without fixtures) as it hung upon a wall at the Dia Foundation: political correctness went right out the window that time. (The urinals, according to the catalog, were meant to represent furtive homosexual liaisons in public toilets—Aids—human plumbing gone bad (?). Frank could have used the museum toilet or gone around the corner to piss against the side of a building—but no, he wanted to address the topic of ART (is it, or isn't it? Only his dealer can tell for sure) directly.

Juan and Jane Birch reappear. Juan is holding a rolled up sleeping bag. Shit! She IS going to camp on my floor!

"Let me know when you're ready to leave," Jane says. "I won't be sleepy for hours."

Next time I look, she is snoozing on the couch, and Kathy BienSur is quizzing me. "Did you call Marie? I told you to call her. It's of the utmost importance."

"I don't feel like calling her."

"Go right into the bedroom and call. I order you to

call." She waves a boney finger in front of my face. "You whose name is scratched in the sands of time must obey me."

"Fuck you Kathy."

I find my way to the bedroom/studio, shove some coats aside, and push telephone buttons. Marie is home. She picks up. The voice I love to hate is in my ear: "Hello?"

I don't answer.

"Hello?"

Kathy opens the door a crack. "Good," she says, seeing that I am on the phone and not getting high (selfishly) by myself. "Ask Marie if she's ever had an abortion. And hurry up so you can introduce me to your new Brit friend. She just might want to lend her support and signature to our cause. Germaine Greer has."

"Marie, it's Julia, I..."

"So, you already know."

"Know what?"

"Josef's going to be on the Geraldo Show."

"Really? What's the topic?"

"Reconciliation—forgiveness."

"With who?" I know it can't be with me.

"Tune in Monday and find out."

"Thanks...for nauseating me."

"You're welcome."

"Tell me already!" Kathy says. She is sitting on the couch, Jane's head in her lap. Jane is munching on a piece of celery.

"Josef's going to be on the Geraldo Show Monday."

"Uh oh..."

"Who's Josef? Who's Geraldo?" Jane asks.

"Josef is someone I'm married to, who is waiting for me to die so he can donate my organs for transplant," I say. "We're living apart at the moment. And Geraldo is a TV talk show host who doesn't know me at all, but if he did, he'd want to fuck me."

Kathy says, "If I had a husband like yours, Julia, I'd do

installations of torture-objects using him to demonstrate their efficiency."

"Would you like to come to my place Monday?" I know Kathy's dying to see my new digs. "I'll make lunch; Jane's staying with me for a few days, so it'll be like a party."

"I'll bring flowers (Kathy, delighted with the idea). What kind do you like?"

"No, please don't bother."

"No bother at all. I have a garden in full bloom."

She has nothing of the sort. She has a Korean fruit and vegetable market around the corner that also sells flowers. Anyway she's a flower person. One would think she'd been a bee in a former life, or a cup of mulch made of fruit peelings.

"I never watch TV," Jane says.

"I can't imagine such a thing; I'd die without TV," I reply.

"Well I guess I'll have to watch it at your place," she concedes, "since I'm to be your guest."

"You did promise to let me interview you," I say.

"Oh yes, my mother thing. It's time I tattled on her...and on him, dear old dad." Sitting bolt upright. "Something's burning."

A candle set upon a work table in the studio has fallen and set fire to a stack of drawings. Juan stands by screaming at Frank, while (The Guy) puts the fire out with a small red fire extinguisher.

"You did it to spite me." Juan yells. "Pack your things and get out."

"My name is on the lease," Frank shouts back. "And besides, I'm dying."

Instant silence. Juan shocked. "You're what?"

"I'm dying."

"Of what?" He staggers toward Frank, arms open, ready to embrace him.

"Your inattention to my needs," a petulant Frank says.

Without a word, Juan smacks Frank, who deserves it. They clean up the mess without another word spoken. I've had it; I slip out with Jane racing after me. So I didn't get to taste Frank's famous pear tarts, or to eat his double-trouble chocolate layer cake. I'll be better off for it.

artfab@mama.ed

Hi Julia. Anyone? Nana again. Went to Joel Journee Gallery in SoHo. Leather and chrome boxes holding flesh-tinted (brown and pink) plastic body parts: hands, heads, penises, feet. Exact renditions of the body masculine distributed in chic artsy containers. Comment please. I'm so repulsed.
AUNTY MAIM KNOWS HIS STUFF.
Then I visited another gallery in the same building, looked up, and saw dozens of stuffed shapeless pink legs in high heels dangling from the ceiling. Lots of tiny balls containing mouthfuls of teeth on the floor. So hazardous. So toony.
IN OLDEN DAYS A GLIMPSE OF STOCKING WAS LOOKED ON AS SOMETHING SHOCKING NOW HEAVEN KNOWS, ANYTHING GOES!
Susan Rothenberg is great even though she's a painter.
PAINTING IS ARCHAIC.
Susan Rothenberg is great even though painting is archaic. You should see her painting of horse's heads/nostrils exchanging breath—like in the Sistine Chapel: fingers touching creating life. It's not really about horses. It's about
LIFE? THAT'S WHAT'S WRONG WITH IT. IT'S HEAVY WITH IMPORT—A PROPHECY FROM MACBETH—AND YOU KNOW WHAT THAT LED TO!
Bloody hands and guilt?
WOMEN'S LIBERATION AND A CENTURY OF BAD PRODUCTIONS.
Really?
YEAH. LADY MACBETH SHOULD HAVE BEEN KING OF THE HILL. SHE WAS THE ONE WANTED IT. SHE HAD THE PASSION.
So what does that have to do with Susan Rothenberg? Gandi Brody has more to do with her. She handles paint like he did. I saw a retrospective of his work last year.

YEAH, I HAPPENED TO SEE THAT SHOW TOO. SEE, HE'D GO
CRAZY IF HE WAS STILL ALIVE. HE WAS SO UNAPPRECI-
ATED. NOT THAT I CARE.
You don't care?
MAYBE I CARE. HEY, I'M SIGNING OFF. GOTTA GO.
Later then.
YEAH.

6

A rectangular, official looking envelope, not to be opened the usual way, arrives; it is perforated on all four sides so as to prevent tampering. I release its narrow borders by tearing the paper carefully, corner to corner. Inside there is a court notice notifying me of a visit in the near future by two city investigators who would like to ask me some questions regarding the rug store fire. The notice says that I may call the number at the bottom of the page for confirmation, or for change of date, time, or place. Hadn't that business been settled in court? Or did they get the wrong man (as The Guy implied)? Happens all the time. I suppose it's important for me to tell them all I know, which isn't much; but I don't trust them—what if they try to implicate me?—What if a neighbor reports that I was seen arguing heatedly with the proprietor the day before the fire? (It was about the carpet I'd bought from him, shedding). I'll bet that Guy I met at Juan's knows more about it than I do, just as he implied.

WHY IS IT THAT STRANGERS KNOW MORE ABOUT ME THAN I DO?

It's really hairy. It's like what John Lennon once said to a friend as they descended from his suite to the lobby of the St.Regis Hotel: "Why is it that strangers know more about me than I do?" Before the friend could reply he'd added: "And why is it that people always give you things when you no longer need 'em?"

Q: There are so many terrible things.
A: Yes, yes, more now than ever.
Q: Everything stinks.
A: The whole world.

Q: This kitchen. I'm doing my best to create a little order.

I take one of those outdated Percodan's with a large glass of water—I'm not sure whether being out of date makes it stronger or absolutely useless, but I have nothing else to calm me down.

"Meditate," Jane says. "Sit in the closet and meditate."

"There's no room in the closet," I answer.

"Make room." She has already pulled her knapsack from the closet and is about to dispossess the three-legged dog.

"Stop it! I don't sit in closets."

"Drink some Camomile tea then."

"There is none."

"I have some in my knapsack."

We drink the tea. She burns her tongue. I bring a cube of ice to cool it.

"I'm ready to be interviewed," she says, "but I'd like a copy of the finished tape for myself. Is that possible? I'll pay for it."

"It's not a matter of payment," I say. "I wouldn't want it showing up somewhere without my knowledge or permission."

"Of course not. I'll put it in writing, for personal use only."

I'm not the Jack Kerouac of video art (untampered with stream of toilet-paper consciousness, drug induced holy-holy wholly holey homo-sclerotic account of the Hard(y)on boys in America). I cut, splice, intercut material from former/stock tapes, add voice-overs, music, strange sounds. Well I have to. Although I don't really have to. I've tried being simple, like talking-heads, but I tend to lean in the direction of more is better. This process takes a long time, sometimes years. My work is ongoing, generative, organic, and never done; it remains as unfinished as the three legged dog with no ribbon.

"Are you sure you're comfortable?" Jane is seated on her rolled up sleeping bag, back against the wall.

"I'm okay for now."

"You can get up and walk around if you want to, stretch,

make a phone call. Won't bother me. I'll keep shooting and asking questions."

"Super."

"Your mother died recently, right?"

"Right—a few months ago she told me that she had decided to die. Actually she went into mourning fifteen years ago when daddy died. Somewhere between that time and the time she made her announcement to me, she stopped going out of the house, stopped dressing other than to change her nightgown—finally she refused to get out of bed. For the last year she wouldn't watch the telly or read the papers. A nurse took care of her...I could use another cup of tea—would you mind putting the kettle on?"

"Were you close to your mother?" I replenish the water in the kettle with some Poland bottled water. It doesn't take long to boil, conceivably because the pot was not watched. A watched pot never boils. Even I slow down when someone watches me. Better to boil unobserved. "Were you close to your mother?" I repeat, carrying the fresh cup of tea to her.

"No. She shut me out," blowing on the tea to cool it. "She only confided in me when she wanted to make me feel bad."

"Such as?"

"When she said that daddy was having an affair with a man—that he dressed up in women's clothing—and that the man daddy was having an affair with was the family lawyer." Pausing to see my reaction. I have none. She continues, "He's the one who is now handling mother's estate. I became ill after that—poor mother blamed herself for daddy's interest in men—thought perhaps she had failed him sexually—what ignorance—so she punished herself—can you imagine that?— She talked about suicide for a long, long time—got the doctor to give her pills to take—and then in the last few months she stopped talking about it. The doctor gave her heavier and heavier shots of morphine—and at the end a huge amount that killed her. The death certificate said something about thrombosis...I could use a cracker and some cheese if you have it," Jane buries her face in her hands speaking into the receptive hollow they make, "...something strong: cheddar or roquefort...I need a protein and fat pick-me-up."

"You don't have to go on if you don't want to." I put the camera down. Take her in my arms. "All I have is Lite low-fat Swiss," I say.

"Fine," she says, continuing to sip the tea; then, her voice rising in anger: "Why didn't the doctor get in touch with me, tell me he was going to kill her off with a final shot of morphine? Why? Did he think we had nothing to say to each other?" Her voice softens, quivering, "Mother never told me that she loved me—maybe at the end she would have."

"And your father?"

"When he died I told him that I knew he was a transvestite. Why do children have to know these things!"

She seems to be shouting at my Lautrec poster of Jane Avril. The one I put up to cover the holes in the wall. Would Avril have been able to answer her question? I make a mental note to look up Jane Avril, her life as an artiste in Paris. Was she anorexic? Did she wear underpants? If she did, were they split up the middle? That's what the Can-Can was all about: catching a glimpse of cunt during the high kicks. Being small of stature (5'1") like Lautrec, was no liability there. They say the first thing he noticed on being introduced to a woman was her nostrils. What was the second?

JANE SHOWS ME A PHOTO OF HERSELF STANDING BESIDE HER MOTHER AND FATHER— HER MOTHER IS SMALLER THAN EITHER OF THEM. JANE HOLDS A MEDAL THAT THE QUEEN HAS PRESENTED TO HER FATHER—ALL ARE VERY PROUD— THE PARENTS DO NOT KNOW THAT JANE IS PREGNANT—HER MOTHER IS TWELVE YEARS OLDER THAN HER FATHER: PALE AND PRIM—THE FATHER IS TALL AND BONY. I WILL USE THIS PHOTOGRAPH BLOWN UP, AND ALSO IN DETAIL,

Rosalyn Drexler

ISOLATING PARTS OF IT: THE MEDAL, A SMILE, A
HAND, THE CASTLE GATE BEHIND THE FAMILY GROUP.

Jane continues. "Mother went through her most cher-
ished possessions with a fine-toothed comb, destroying or
giving them away to an ungrateful parade of part-time
housekeepers and nurses, leaving nothing for me, at least
nothing I'd want to hold on to as a keepsake, no memento
of our mother/daughter life together; not even a letter, or
a birthday card. However, I did find the queen's medal
lying on top of some items in a drawer—for years I believed
that I'd lost it, and suffered the most unimaginable guilt.
Mum let me believe it, and so, in time I did believe it and
did become that uncaring, undependable, selfish daughter
she had invented; the one who had borrowed the family
treasure and lost it."

VOICE OVER
Birthing scene in cemetery.
JANE WROTE THE VICAR WHO OFFICIATED AT HER
MOTHER'S MEMORIAL SERVICE A LETTER THANKING HIM
FOR RAISING THE QUALITY OF THE SERVICE ABOVE THE
BANAL (EVEN THOUGH HE'D HAD A BIT TOO MUCH TO
DRINK) BY DECLARING "ALL OF US ARE BORN OF WOMAN,"
INSTEAD OF THE USUAL "MAN IS BORN OF WOMAN."

VICAR
(tipsy)
All of us are born of woman,
for which there is no forgiveness.
There should be other ways to arrive
here: men drive buses don't they?
So why not give men a chance! Birth
my friends, is merely a matter of
negotiating that slick orgasmic water
slide into life's teeming pool of
slop and waste. Let's help modern science

get woman out of the stirrups that bind
her, and let's support the humane notion that
men can be as useful in a petrie dish, as
they have been in a woman. Dear ones, I for
one have always been for a fair division of
labors. Let us now pray.

Jane avoids me after the interview. She feels that she has
betrayed a trust—her own. She spends the next three days out:
visiting with her agent, her publisher, discussing magazine
articles with editors, shopping, etc. I try to think. Can't.
Wonder what I'm going to do to lift this interview out of the
ordinary. I consider inviting some of my more outrageous
(screaming queens) friends to be in the video. ("There she goes/
Miss Brittanica.") Intercut Jane's wrenching question, "Why
do children have to know these things?" with the question,
"Are we having fun yet?"

WHY DO CHILDREN HAVE TO KNOW
THESE THINGS?

They don't have to know these things. The sexual
misconduct of parents should be their own business. It's
definitely impolite for a father to visit a child's school on
visitors day, dressed (as his mother) in skirt and high heels.

ARE WE HAVING FUN YET?
Quotes gathered from numerous gay tabloids
"Yes."
"No."
"Maybe."

7

Today's Monday, the day I am going to watch Josef on the Geraldo Show. I should be relieved; at least I'll know where he is (not waiting for me around the corner, or hiding on the roof, eager to drop a brick on my head when Officer Pup isn't looking—that li'l dollin'). I am wearing a new blouse (as if dressed for a date). It's sheer cotton with cap sleeves. There is a small square of paper in the breast pocket (the left one). I read the message, holding the paper away from my face. The print is very small. It says: Inspected by #5. Number five your name is legion and your surveillance ever vigilant. I am grateful to Number Five for seeing to it that my garment has no tears, crooked seams, or buttons missing. Who is she? Is she a he? Maybe. And maybe whoever it is, is an underpaid immigrant hurrying through her daily quota, trying to increase her productivity to make more money. #5 and I should meet; have a fast lunch standing up at a street stand: horse meat on a spit, soda pop, Good Humor bar. Lots of girl talk. Worlds apart. Me, free to wander. #5, in a rush to get back to her machine.

DOCU-SOCIOLOGICAL-VIDEO-ADVENTURE-EXAMINING THE NEW IMMIGRANTS

The squalid world of present day sweatshops.
The comraderie of the women.
The constant whirr of sewing machines.
The piles of garments.
Interviews with the workers: their lives and aspirations.
FIND A MIDDLE GROUND BETWEEN THE GENIUS SENSIBILITY OF A JOHN LEGUIZAMO (TOUGH, FUNNY, CHARACTER STUDIES) AND THE CLEVER/BOTH SIDES OF

THE PICTURE CHARACTERIZATIONS OF ANN DEAVERE SMITH. USE ANIMATION TO ILLUSTRATE POINTS IN THE STYLE OF PUBLIC SCHOOL EDUCATIONAL FILMS, THE ONES THAT TEACH YOU HOW TO BRUSH YOUR TEETH. I have used thoughts about #5 to allay my anxiety concerning Josef on TV. Will he trash me in public? Will I be mentioned at all? Why does Krazy Kat continue to love Ignaz the Mouse when he knows that Ignaz lives to conk him with a brick?

"Don't worry about it," Kathy says. "Whatever he says may be used against him."

Jane puts on the TV. Switches to channel 2.

"Not bad looking," she says.

"Who?" I ask.

"That guy with the viva Zapata moustache."

"That's Geraldo," Kathy says, "a real jerk. You'll see."

"Josef isn't on yet." I say.

Geraldo talks about what to expect on today's show: the quality of mercy—forgiveness—confrontation—the opportunity for abused and abuser to express what they feel. He alerts the audience that not even "J" (he calls Josef "J" in order to preserve his anonymity) knows who will be behind the curtain confessing to dastardly deeds and begging for pardon.

Josef is seated beside Marie. She tells the story of how Dwayne, J's stepfather beat Josef into insensibility at the age of five, because the child could only recite the alphabet up to the letter H.

"Dwayne has been punished for it," she says. "He knows he done wrong and he'd like for everyone to give him another chance."

Josef is visibly upset. He clenches and unclenches his fists. His face reddens. He crosses and uncrosses his legs.

"I'd like to say something," Josef says, "but I can't."

Geraldo, determined not to be miffed, smiles. "I think I can help you," he says (voice rising in anger). "Perhaps you want to tell us that DWAYNE is a CHILD ABUSER and

SADISTIC FREAK who gets his jollys off by attacking those weaker than he is. (professionally suave) Let's see what Dwayne has to say about this," gesturing upstage. "Ladies and gentlemen, Mr. Dwayne Konrad!"

The audience does not know how to behave: applaud or not? Dwayne is a guest, isn't he? On the other hand he's a bad guy, isn't he? The applause is scanty and hesitant.

Dwayne takes a seat at the far end of the row of chairs. He is dressed in newly washed "work clothes" his hair is slicked back, his face clean shaven, the tattoo of a tiger on his left forearm is exposed below a rolled up shirt sleeve. I can see that the man has taken extra care with his appearance; when else will he be seen by an audience of millions? Who knows what will come of it? Marriage proposals? Job offers? Book rights? He's even bought a new pair of boots with fancy silver tips, and wears a beaded Indian tie. TV brings out the best in people, I think.

"That's a weird guy," Kathy says. "Looks like he shaves with sandpaper."

"Dwayne, do you have anything to say to 'J' ?"

Dwayne straightens his tie. His jaw juts forward, "Wasn't for him I wouldn't of had to do time. Stubborn little sucker, wanted to come between me and Marie. First he wouldn't use his potty, and we had to clean him up—I got past that, but it sure grossed me out—took it kind of personal—then no matter how hard I tried he wouldn't learn the alphabet—kid hated me—I lost it—that's the story in a nutshell."

"I see, unfinished emotional business," Geraldo says. Turning to Josef, "Let's get back to 'J'. Now's your chance 'J', you have a golden opportunity to settle this man to man. What do you say?"

Josef rises slowly, walks toward Dwayne.

The audience, hoping for the best in spite of the look of distress on Josef's face, begins to applaud—this time the applause is sincere and wholehearted.

"I think they're gonna shake hands and call it a day, folks," Geraldo laughs happily, disaster momentarily deferred.

Ann Birch takes my hand, squeezes it. "I can't believe this," she says, "it goes against the laws of nature."

"Well, it's not nature, it's TV" I say.

Marie follows her son, tottering behind him on high heeled shoes: "Stop him," she pleads, "somebody please stop him!"

FUCKUP CITY! There's no stopping Josef. The cameramen concentrate behind their cameras, ready to swivel in any direction; the director and engineers remain (fascinated) within their glassed-in eyrie, safer than anyone else in the studio; a handful of faithful ushers remain at their posts guarding the aisles; while a lone security man stands at the rear exit speaking to his liaison by way of a handheld intercom. They are professional; they are on the alert!

Geraldo, in the audience, carries his cordless "mike" close to his mouth, lips brushing the dark gray foam that covers it; he is sensitive to the situation, ready to interject comment. He tugs at his vest, setting it neatly above his waist: a nervous gesture repeated more than once since the vest will not stay in place. Just then there is a program break.

"Back in a minute folks," Geraldo says cheerfully. "Stay tuned."

Interrupting for a commercial message has about the same effect on the progress of the show as pushing an infant's head back into the vaginal canal when it wants to be born. A commotion is heard but not seen.

"God knows what's gonna happen while the commercial is on," I say. "Could be murder."

Ann and Kathy have a good laugh. "At least it won't be you," Ann says.

During the interval, Personal Mortgage Company offers loans to people who can't get them elsewhere; the five o'clock news attempts to keep the audience glued to their sets with a fast run-down of topics to be covered: the imminent garbage disposal strike; the promised revelation of gruesome keepsakes discovered at the beautifully landscaped home of a serial killer; the station's personally investigated list of tourist traps to avoid. The commercials continue with a furniture sale at Huffman Koos, and a movie ad pushing Tina Turner's life(!) as portrayed in "What's Love Got To Do With It?"

Enough time to break out the salsa and light tortilla chips. Serve the Nutra-Sweet(ened) iced tea. Since Ann's been with me I've had more tea than I care to own up to. And in deference to our new friend, Kathy has added tea-leaf readings to her repertoire; she professes to see "all" in their soggy, clotted arrangement at the bottom of an English bone-ware cup, purchased ("one of a kind") for this purpose from an antiques dealer.

"It's for amusement purposes only," she cautions. "At least until I get the hang of it."

Suddenly we're back again with Geraldo, his face and torso leaning toward us in medium closeup, intimately:

"He's been beaten, kicked, stabbed, left for dead, and yet he is ready to forgive his stepdad," an upbeat Geraldo declares. Then to Josef, 'J' you okay?"

"He's not, he's not!" Marie gasps. "Stop him!"

Too late. The audience is on its feet shreiking. Geraldo is racing for the stage.

"Haven't seen anything so bloody mad since 'The Singing Detective'," Ann says. "It's so exciting."

Josef, knife in hand is yelling: "I! I!"

I, THE LETTER THAT COMES AFTER H!

HE'S GOT IT. JOSEF'S BEEN CURED OF HIS LEARNING DISABILITY. REVENGE IS SWEET. THE SHADOW THAT HAD A HUMAN SHAPE HAS BEEN REMOVED. TODAY THE ALPHABET. TOMORROW THE WORLD!

"Ai yi yi!" Geraldo cries, shaking his head in disbelief as security police burst through the door of the studio, racing for the stage. They pinion Josef's arms behind his back, cautioning him not to make a move. He doesn't fight them, he's lost in word heaven, he speaks words!

"MURMUROUS HEART! MELLIFLUOUS MOTHER!

SORROWFUL SEX!"

Dwayne is removed on a stretcher: noone knows if he's dead or alive. Immediately the station goes to a commercial, leaving us all in the dark. Is Dwayne really dead? Has Marie fainted? Will this exceptional event get Josef off my ass for good? Or will it be like a joke Juan once told me: "A guy with a chicken on his head goes to see a psychiatrist. Is there something I can do for you, the psychiatrist asks? Yeah, the chicken answers, you can get this guy off my ass!" Is Josef the chicken on my head who thinks I'M stalking HIM?

"It'll be on the news," Kathy says. "What a shot in the arm for Geraldo, pure adrenalin—don't see people killing each other on the Oprah, or Donahue Shows. Not that I care. I don't care at all—only did I happen to mention to you that once I was invited to be on the Donahue Show? Yeah, like he wanted to have maybe five psychics on at once, giving their predictions for the new year. At the time I wasn't in a predicting state of mind; it can happen: I was depending on my mood ring to tell me how I felt—that's how bad it was."

"He was a quiet fellow, kept to himself," a neighbor says. Another neighbor intervenes: "You never know. Can't be too careful." The reporter segues to the killer's mother, Marie Konrad; she is standing in the street trying to unlock the door to her apartment house. "Mrs.Konrad, Mrs.Konrad is it true that your son is..." "On the counsel of my lawyer I am advised to remain silent." She slams the door behind her leaving the reporter to his own devises. He promises a discussion on child abuse and its after-effects by a panel of experts, to follow the news.

DWAYNE IS DEFINITELY DEAD

Dwayne is dead. The public doesn't know what to believe... talk show hosts invite pop psychologists to air their diverse and sometimes off the wall opinions, newspaper journalists conservative on the whole, are divided as to whether Dwayne actually attacked the young Josef, or whether it is a case of psychiatrist induced false-memory return. Some call Josef a vicious killer (born to kill), others say he was a time bomb waiting to go off (same thing). "You can't take the law into your own hands," a neighborhood laundromat operator declares. "This is America."

The lawyer who takes cases no other lawyer will touch, Nukler, has agreed to represent Josef. It's a matter of time before the press finds out that I am Josef's wife. Also a matter of time before Marie sells her story to a magazine or TV program.

This is also a perfect opportunity for me to replenish the exchequer; that is, if I dare come forward. So much easier for me to tape strangers; to screw around with their stories, to make them into art—but the use of my own story, or part of my own story is daunting since it would have to refer back to my relationship with Josef: there's more to me than Josef. However, as far as the world is concerned JOSEF is all there is: he has become a sympathetic character; one who was abused, but who has returned to exact a terrible punishment from his tormentor. Suddenly millions of people are familiar with his name and face, recognize his mother Marie from newspaper photos and talk show appearances. She has become as much a celebrity as her son because she is the one who yelled, "Stop him! Stop him!" on national TV. A phrase that is now as popular as "I've fallen and I can't get up," used to be.

Marie has sent me two prayers to help me get through the long days and nights without Josef.

MIO CROCIFISSO!

SEMPRE TI PORTO CON ME.
A TUTTO TI PREFERISCO.
QUANDO CADO, TU MI RISOLLEVI.
QUANDO PIANGO, TU MI CONSOLI.
QUANDO SOFFRO, TU MI QUARISCI.

QUANDO TI CHIAMO, TU MI RISPONDI.

MIO CROCIFISSO!

Sii TU MIA DIFESA IN VITA.
MIO CONFORTO E FIDUCIA,
NELLA MIA AGONIA.
E RIPOSA SUL MIO CUORE,
QUANDO SARA LA MIA ULTIMA ORA.

(da una poesia francese)
(con approvazione ecclesiastica)

8

INSTANT INSANITY

Murder by reason of instant insanity? That's not possible. I once played INSTANT INSANITY; you buy this toy, all of its parts fit perfectly into their niches to make a multi-faceted sphere of sorts, the pieces of this sphere have vari-colored surfaces. When you take the sphere apart you think it will be easy to put it together again, but it doesn't work that way. It takes hours and hours to make it whole again, if ever. Trying to make something whole again can drive one mad.

MURDER BY REASON OF INSANITY

Legal insanity is different than the kind of insanity that keeps one locked away inside oneself forever. Legal insanity comes as a breath of fresh amnesia: "I didn't know what I was doing." Not knowing is the same as: didn't do, wasn't there, am not responsible.

Josef used to say, under his breath of course, so that it would be hard for me to catch what he was saying: "IF I COULD KILL HIM I'D DIE HAPPY."

"Who?"

"Nobody you know."

"Nobody dies happy."

"I would."

ALL IS...ALL IS...ALL IS WHAT? IN A WORD...CORPSED (Sam)

Stan Baltimore is showing his true colors, that of a sex driven provocateur.

"Julia, you owe me this month's rent."

"Check's in the mail."

"My cousin sent me a crate of oranges from Florida, would you like some? They'll only rot on me."

"Squeeze 'em."

"I'd like to squeeze you."

"Yeah?"

"Yeah—hey wanna hear a joke?"

"No."

"This guy goes to a psychiatrist. He says, Doc I have a problem: I have five penises. That is a problem, the psychiatrist says. How do your pants fit? Like a glove, the man replies."

"You just had to say penis, didn't you Stan?"

"Yeah," he admits.

I hang up on him.

He calls back immediately. "I have automatic repeat dialing," he says. "Say, you been following that Geraldo story; I mean about the guy who killed another guy on camera?"

"Go away Stan, I'm busy. Something is taking its course."

"Sure. Why didn't you say so."

Q: Did you ever have an instant of happiness?
A: Not to my knowledge.

JUAN CALLS "Take my advice," Juan says, "never eat anything bigger than your head."

"Even if I take small bites?" What is he talking about?

"Frank's left me," he says, breaking down, "he's gone to Seattle where it rains all the time. He likes that. He likes lush foliage. What am I going to do without him?"

"He'll be back."

"Not this time."

"What can I tell you. Hang tough."

"Thanks...You going to have a preview showing of the skeleton tapes for friends?"

"I'm not ready."

"Let me know when."

"I will."

MANTENGASE EN LA LINEA. SI NO PUEDE LINEA QUEDARSE EN LA LINEA, DELE A LA OPERADORA LA DIRECCION DONDE HACE FALTA AYUDA.

The number I am calling happens to be the U.S. Secret Service. It's the number written on the letter I received regarding the continuing investigation of the fire, asking for an appointment with me. I'd thought it was a city matter. I leave my phone number after the signal, and wait. U.S. Secret Service? That'a beep and a bop! Turns out I misdialed. Got 911. Concerning the incendio, I want to forget it.

This time I dial the correct number. Make the appointment.

They are not wearing raincoats. They have come to see me wearing bright Hawaiian shirts. Someone must have advised them on what to wear when interrogating an artist: something with bright colors—put the sucker at ease. I'm pretty comfortable. I sit in the wheelchair. They sit on two old wooden kitchen chairs I found in the street the other day. Our conversation begins the polite Japanese way (they are not Japanese), not mentioning the reason for their visit.

"You have wheelchair access here?" one of them asks.

He thinks I am non-ambulatory—wheelchair bound—a physically challenged person who enjoys talking about Me and my Pal the Wheelchair: rails for the handicapped on bathroom walls, hydraulic lifts on buses, traveling through the world alone with nothing but a knapsack and a net bag attached to the back of my chair. Who knows what they think?

"There's enough space here. I can race forward, backwards, turn around." I demonstrate the chair's capabilities while they scrape their chairs out of the way, to avoid me.

"You ever tried out for the Special Olympics?" asked by the shorter detective who stares at me through thick lensed glasses.

"I'm not that special," I answer. "I'm really just your ordinary run-of-the-mill paraplegic."

"Sorry; hope I haven't stepped on your toes." He polishes his glasses with a lens tissue. "Acuravision, super soft tissues," he says. "So, you sure I haven't insulted you?"

"I'm used to it," I say. "Unless you've walked a mile in my shoes there's no way you could know the right thing to say to me."

The first detective, Mr. Palm Trees (illustrated on his shirt) shows me a photograph. "Ever see this man?"

"Yeah," I say, "he looks familiar."

"How familiar?"

"Well maybe the word familiar is the wrong word."

"Yeah?"

"Familiar implies closeness, a relationship." I shrug, not wanting to reveal The Guy's identity.

"Try casual." The shorter detective, Mr. Flamingo (illustrated on his shirt), says.

"Yeah, he looks casual," I say.

"Casual? Guy's a bad egg. Bad eggs are never casual. They stink." Mr. Flamingo says. "You smell anything funny in here?" to his sidekick.

"I'm a terrible housekeeper," I say, before Mr. Palm Trees can sniff around. "Always forget to take the garbage out."

"We're only trying to do our job," Mr. Palm Trees says, ignoring the talk about bad smells and garbage. Speaking in a persuasive tone: "This guy is a hardened criminal. You can help us put him where he belongs."

"I'm sorry, I can't help you," I say decisively.

"Well, if you change your mind, call us."

I walk them to the door.

They're amazed at my sudden recovery.

"It's a miracle," I say. "Thank you."

"Think nothing of it," Mr. Flamingo replies. "In another life I was Jesus Christ."

70

SOUNDING THE ALARM

I dial The Guy's number immediately. First ring he picks up. Guy must live by the phone: "I think we should meet," I say. "Two detectives have been here asking about you. They showed me a photograph of you."

"I knew it. I've been looking everywhere for that picture. What a disaster."

"Just because they have a picture of you?"

"I've looked better."

"So, you coming over?"

"Got a few things to take care of first."

"Get here as soon as you can."

I set up the video camera: this time on a tripod. If there is a confession, I want to get it on tape. The Guy is so vain he'll trust me completely.

9

GUY'S DELIGHT—AN INTERVIEW

Q: When did you first know that you were homosexual?
A: What has that got to do with my wonderful career?
(Disappointed)

Q: Forget it for now. Next question. Those detectives say you're a hardened criminal; true or not? Didn't you say you had secret information about the fire? Or was that just a come-on?

A: They think I'm a HARDENED criminal? Oh my dear, how flattering! (He pulls at his pony tail.) Now that I have this Spanish "do" I'll have to learn to dance the Tango.

Q: Come on, stop kidding around; when was it you first realized you were homosexual? This is valuable information. You could be helping other men who need role models: there are suicidal teenagers out there, demeaning fathers, rejecting mothers, teasing sisters, violent brothers, unhelpful teachers, useless legislators, psychologists with their own agenda!

A: Okay I'll talk—When I was five years of age I sensed that I was different: tried on my Aunt Lorraine's art-deco necklace and wouldn't give it back. Cried bitter tears when they finally tore it from me: even then, at that tender age I was crazy about fashion. I could have been Coco Chanel, that is if SHE hadn't been Coco Chanel. When I was six I discovered hair curlers and bobby pins: a discovery as important to me as finding a dinosaur embryo is to a paleontologist. Had a collection of old movie magazines. Wanted to look like Shirley Temple, but resembled Jane Withers, you know, the homely, sassy kid with the braids. Before our time, my dear. It was so glamorous then. My period is the thirties and forties, into the early fifties. Used to be the twenties. Soon, if I don't watch out it'll be the sixties. They're comparing the sixties to the twenties! Can you believe it? Well, way before puberty, I was introduced to mutual masturabation by a school chum. What I remember best about it is the echoing, hollow sound we made as our activities bounced off the tiled walls of the boys toilet, and the smell!—Phew! Once I got the hang of it I seduced my brother, taught him to play my "games." Every night I'd creep into his bed for comfort, which is how I became addicted to adorable **PEONIES**; my code name for penises. **PEONIES**: heavy, smooth, arching gracefully on their thick moist stems. (Agitated) It all comes back to me now...my beloved brother finally refusing to play with me...mother throwing a tantrum because I wouldn't eat. When she sent brother away to boarding school, I was devastated. I had no other friends. My happiest diversion was dressing up the neighbor's dog in bonnet and pinafore which I made from an old tablecloth. Before I could win his approval, daddy died. Heart attack. Now whenever I hear the words, "HEART AT-TACK!" I think that a huge heart shaped Valentine's Day box of chocolates that was on the coffee table the day he died, hurled itself at daddy and killed him. Cheap chocolates are inevitably malevolent, don't you agree?

Q: How could you stand it?

A: Couldn't. Years later I tried to kill myself by eating a five pound box of candy: the Whitman's Sampler with co-deine on the side, and a bottle of rum. S'funny, made me feel almost good. I have such a strong constitution I'd have to sit on a land mine to kill myself. So I picked myself up, dried my tears and took a course in fabric design at the Parsons School of Design instead, where I was finally recognised as a considerable talent by my professors.

Q: When you graduated did the school help you find a job?

A: They recommended me to a few big companies; took a while for me to be hired of course, but when I was hired, ZOWEE! Right off I began designing a new line, my own, just like Gloria Vanderbilt. I was a great success until I was fired.

Don't ask me why.
   Q: Why?
   A: Don't ask me why.
   Q: Why?
   A: Have you seen The Crying Game?
   Q: Yes.
   A: Were you surprised when the secret was revealed? When the "woman" opened her robe and you saw, without a doubt, that the she was a he?
   Q: No. Her/his legs gave him away: knobby-kneed, muscled, sinewy—hips no wider than a thigh. Lipstick, eye-makeup, wigs, padding, dress, and high heels can't conceal the truth. Actually the truth isn't in the look, it's in the smell. Women give off different pheromones than men. Never in the movies though. In the movies everything smells like popcorn.
   A: Excuse me? What's a pheronome?
   Q: It's a phobic thing: FEAR OF GNOMES. Happens without warning in women of childbearing age.
   A: Oh, then women have something to do with fairy tale characters? Phenomenal! I believe in fairies, don't you? (pause) What kind of a traitor would I be if I didn't? (pause) Getting back to me, cross dressing really relaxes me: brings out the sweetness within. That's why I was fired. You think things have changed in the world? They haven't.
   Q: No?
   A: Not for queers.
   Q: So what.
   A: So pain.
   Q: You're not the only one.
   A: I AM the only one.
   Q: What do you know about the fire?
   A: (He lights a cigarette) My exclusive designs began to appear on cheap stuff everywhere: Conway's, Sears, K Mart, Lamston's. I didn't have a pot to piss in, yet others were profiting from my efforts. I'd lost my cachet. Was invited nowhere. I was going crazy.

Q: How crazy?

A: I wanted to destroy what had been stolen from me—to get rid of every cheap imitation in existence.

Q: So what did you do?

A: I didn't have the kind of money it takes to fight the big corporations in court—so I took matters into my own hands—set fire to whatever I could.

Q: The rug and floor-coverings store? You did it?

A: Yes, it was a matter of revenge.

Q: Then you're not sexually excited by fire?

A: If anything, fire makes me ill. I hate to sweat, and smoke makes me nauseous.

Q: Are you going to turn yourself in?

A: Not when I have two first class tickets to Brazil. It's Mardigras time baby! How'd you like to join me?

THE COLLAR

The detectives know all. They've been listening to The Guy (real name Dick Gull) and me on a hidden device. He is collared as he leaves my domicile. It's goodbye Mardigras, goodbye Brazil for him. I was going to call and offer him Mr. J.G.O.'s address and phone number, which I forgot to do when he was here. However he no longer has any use for Brazilian introductions, does he? On thinking it over (his unsolicited confession to me, his apprehension, his altogether unpleasant intrusion into my life), I sincerely believe that the detectives have picked up the wrong man. It was too easy. Dick (a.k.a. The Guy) must be protecting someone. The man is a marshmallow (that's obvious), and marshmallows don't welcome being toasted in a fire no matter how delicious they taste to us campers.

SPYING DEVICE

It takes me a while to find the "bug." I look in the lamp, behind the sink, over the door, in the phone—then I find it—the detectives have stuck it under the seat of one of the straight backed chairs as if it were a piece of chewed Wrigley's Spearmint gum.

artfab@mama.ed

Hannah Wilke used to put these cunt shaped pieces of chewed gum on museum walls. Then she put some on her face to make it look like scars, that's what I read, but it was before my time. Feminist art is so obviously cunty and uninspired, yet in just the space of a few years it's begun to attract serious consideration among the cognoscenti.

COUNT ME OUT. I'M NOT A FAN. BUT HANNAH WAS ANOTHER KETTLE OF FISH: STARIFICATION/SCARIFICA- TION. I'M SURE SHE CHEWED TILL THE FLAVOR WAS GONE. HER PHOTOGRAPHS OF HER DYING MOTHER AND AFTERWARDS OF HERSELF DYING OF CANCER WERE REMARKABLE. A NAKED HANNAH WAS AS MOVING IN HER OWN WAY AS A NAKED AGING ALICE NEEL.

I don't want to be reminded that my body is deteriorating, that I am dying. Death stay away from my door. Catch you later, Julia.

COWARD!

10

I've just returned from shopping at Gristede's with a cooked Tyson chicken, a head of lettuce, a loaf of seven grain bread, and a bunch of red seedless grapes. As I put the food into the refrigerator I sense that something is amiss: can't put my finger on it. Oh well, it's probably my imagination. No, it's not. The smell is missing: that indefinable, intrusive odor of rot has disappeared.

The windows are not open. The trash cans still in their niche. On a hunch I lift the lid of one can—look inside—no skeleton. I look into the other trash can—the skeleton is gone from that one too. Now I'm scared—someone has been here. Juan? He's the only one I know who's interested in skeletons.

WHAT'S HAPPENING?

The phone rings. It's Stan Baltimore.

"I had to let them in," he says. "They had a search warrant."

"You have keys to my place?" I'm horrified.

"It's the law; the landlord has to have a set of keys in case of an emergency. So I have 'em."

"So who did you let in?"

"Detectives. Didn't leave 'em alone for a second; made sure they didn't take anything—just them two skeletons. They were real interested in them."

"Thanks for letting me know," I say. I'm shaking. I'll have to put in a new lock, one that Stan Baltimore won't get the key to. However, what good is locking the barn door after the cow has gone?

77

11

There's a knock at the door. I'm unprepared for it—open the door without asking who it is—in rolls Hamm seated in a motorized wheelchair, wearing a pair of customized wraparound sun glasses.

"I thought you weren't coming back," I say.

"Who told you that?"

"Stan Baltimore."

"Doesn't know his ass from his elbow macaroni. I've returned to pay a visit to my parents. You've met them I take it?"

"They're dead," I say, "nothing but bones."

"I suppose you think I killed them?"

"Are you telling me you didn't?"

"If they have died, it was a natural death. Anyone forced to live in a galvanized trash can would die, naturally. But I did feed them Peak Freens and ginger biscuits. They hated broccoli. Wouldn't eat meat. How could they with no teeth? Before I lost my eyesight I was a painter; painted a still life entitled: TEETH BITING WATER IN A GLASS. Anniversary present for my parents. What a love story! Where are they? (taking out a box of crackers) Brought one last treat."

"They've been taken away by the police."

OUR REVELS NOW ARE ENDED

"They'll accuse me of abusing the elderly. Of contributing to the death of my parents. What defense do I have? That they would have died sooner had I left them alone in some cold flat? Father? (Frightened, calling) Father speak to me. You are my only hope...Even the dog is gone."

"Actually it's not," I say. "It's right here."

"Give him to me."
I hand the dog to Hamm. He throws it down.
"You don't want him?"
"Don't like the way he feels. I want daddy and mommy."
"If it's any comfort at all, they spoke well of you."
"What exactly did they say? Did they complain that even though I am blind I refuse to play harmonica for them?"
"Your daddy said he would have liked to hear you call him like when you were a tiny boy, and were frightened, in the dark, and he was your only hope."
"Father! (pause) Father! I'm coming," he calls plaintively.
As he wheels his chair out of my apartment, he says, "You've done wonders with this place. Look at all this beauty. This order! (sadly) You ought to know what the earth is like, nowadays."
"I do," I say, "when there is no food, the heart eats itself."
He tears a harmonica from his T-shirt pocket, tosses it to me, "With my compliments. Nothing to keep me here now."
"I don't know any tunes to play," I protest.
"You just put your lips together and blow."
"Like this?" As if by magic, very soft magic, I play "As Time Goes By."
("Julia, I thought I told you never to play it!")
MED. SHOT—BECKETT—ACCOMPANYING ME AT THE PIANO

79

12

A SEXY LETTER

Dear Julia,

I want to thank you for providing the highlight of my trip to America. I have not been able to forget you. You were so kind, so feminine, so open that I feel we are already friends. One must not keep anything from a friend, right? Therefore, I consider it an honor and a duty to tell you what happened to me on my return home. If it is too intimate, and makes you blush, I give you my permission to destroy this letter; however, I hope you will not.

As I usually do on the weekend, I was working in the barn, tending to the cows, when my daughter-in-law came to call me in for lunch. She was wearing a very lowcut blouse, so low cut that her red nipples surrounded by a large brownish halo were revealed to me. Yes, her titties were as firm as the distended udders of a cow with too much milk. A fly, there are so many horse flys here, landed on her bosom, and without thinking I brushed it off, letting my hand linger on that compact hill of flesh; her breasts were as firm as a pair of buttock's cheeks, I do not lie, and as I fondled them I could have sworn they were a young girl's behind. The moment was so delightful that I entirely forgot she was my son's wife. She certainly did not object to my attentions for we had a tacit agreement to enjoy the experience come what may. Yes, perhaps I am a bit of a mind reader. I then leisurely kissed her nipples. She smelled of sweat, in a way that excited me. It was that odor di femina which emanates from a woman's body, that I eagerly inhaled. Then she unzipped my fly, revealing my member in a state of huge excitement: large and firm, the cap was already a purplish red, and the tip wet with a preliminary whitish goo. The naughty girl couldn't take her eyes off of my sexual parts. She was by now sitting on a mound of fragrant hay, leaning back with eyes closed, and lips parted. My state of excitement was excruciating, the least touch would have made me come. I lifted her dress, and saw a pair of thighs which fired my enthusiasm even more. Between the closed thighs I caught sight of a small tangle of chestnut-colored hairs, among which her reddish crack was concealed.

Overwhelmed by desire I dropped to my knees, seized her thighs, let my hands roam caressingly everywhere, laid my cheeks upon them and covered them with kisses. My wet lips advanced from the thighs to her venus mound where the smell of urine only added fuel to my excitement. I had to go on or die, even though we were now in danger of being discovered; surely someone else was being sent to see why we were not at the afternoon repast.

I must end this letter now since I hear my wife approaching, but you will be receiving another one in the near future, one that continues to detail the secret story of my joyous folly and subsequent downfall. Please write to me, let me know how you are, and whether you too have amorous adventures.

Yours,
Juvenal

P.S. Please send all correspondence to my factory: Companhia Grupo Nacional, AVENIDA AMERANTE BARROSO 10 Rio de Janeiro, RJ Brazil. If for any reason you need a load of steel, I'm your man. Dear Julia, you must come to Brazil: you will not get cholera or dysentry I promise, but you will sing and dance and go to theater. I will be your escort. A very proper one, have no fear.

"The man is a pervert," Kathy says. "I'll bet that somewhere in this world there's a half-human, half-bovine creature mooing for its daddy. He's setting you up."

WANTED: PARENTS FOR CALF-BABY

BEFORE THIS CALF-BABY IS PUT OUT TO PASTURE, HIS HEARTBROKEN MOM, JULIA THE COW, IS MAKING ONE LAST ATTEMPT TO PLACE HIM IN A HOME WITH LOVING PARENTS.

"I KNOW WHO HIS FATHER IS, BUT I GUESS HE'LL NEVER OWN UP TO IT. THEY SAY THAT THERE WAS A MIX-UP AT THE ANIMAL HUSBANDRY SPERM BANK. THAT'S A LOT OF BULL! AFTER BEING TOLD BY FERTILITY SPECIALISTS THAT I WOULD NEVER BRING FORTH CALVES, MY OWNER MR. J.G.O. OFFERED HIS OWN SPERM, THE SPERM OF A HUMAN BEING, AND IT WORKED. MY SON WAS BORN WITH A HUMAN BODY AND A COW'S FACE. HE REALLY IS A WONDERFUL LITTLE CALF, FRISKY, PLAYFUL: I HATE TO GIVE HIM UP, BUT IT WILL BE BEST FOR HIM IN THE LONG RUN."

THE OWNER MR. J.G.O. SAID, "PRECAUTIONS SHOULD HAVE BEEN TAKEN. THERE ARE SUCH THINGS AS CONDOMS. IF A CONDOM HAD BEEN USED, TRAGEDY MIGHT HAVE BEEN AVERTED. WHOEVER DID THIS THING HAS TAKEN ADVANTAGE OF ONE OF GOD'S POOR DEFENSELESS CREATURES! HE IS AN EVIL, HEARTLESS, COWARD WHO DESERVES PUNISHMENT. JUST LET ME CATCH HIM! HE'LL WISH HE WERE DEAD!"

ACCORDING TO THE VET IN ATTENDANCE, THE PREGNANCY WAS UNEVENTFUL AND NOBODY REALIZED ANYTHING HAD GONE WRONG UNTIL THEY HEARD MOOING SOUNDS COMING FROM THE INFANT IN THE CRECHE.

"MY ASSISTANT SAID TO ME: 'OH MY GOD, THAT CALF LOOKS LIKE A BABY!'

"WE WHISKED THE NEWBORN MUTANT FROM THE BARN AND PLACED HIM IN A LOCKED ROOM IN OUR OWN HOSPITAL WHERE WE COULD OBSERVE HIM IN SECRECY. HIS MOTHER, OF COURSE, WAS ALLOWED TO STAY WITH HIM IN ORDER TO FULFILL HER MOTHERLY DUTIES OF NURSING AND LICKING HIM TO SLEEP."

AT FIRST JULIA DID ALL SHE COULD TO BRING THE
CALF 'ROUND. BUT WHEN ALL HE DID WAS LIE ON HIS
BACK AND KICK HIS LEGS IN THE AIR, SHE BECAME
NASTY TOWARD HIM AND REFUSED TO NURSE HIM.
THE VETS CONSULTED WITH A TEAM OF PLASTIC
SURGEONS ASSOCIATED WITH THE MAYO CLINIC WHO
SAID THEY'D BE ABLE TO PERFORM PLASIC SURGERY ON
HIM. TO EVERYONE'S MIND THE BABY WAS A FREAK
WITHOUT A FUTURE UNLESS HE WAS OPERATED ON.
MR. J.G.O., AFTER CONSULTING WITH JULIA AND
THE MEDICAL STAFF, AND AFTER A LOT OF SOUL SEARCH-
ING AND PRAYER, DECIDED TO HELP JULIA IN HER
DECISION TO PLACE THE CALF-BABY FOR ADOPTION:
THE INFANT WOULD NEED LOTS OF ATTENTION AND
LOVING CARE BEFORE, DURING, AND AFTER THE
OPERATIONS. INDEED, IT MIGHT TAKE MANY OPERA-
TIONS AND MANY YEARS BEFORE THE CHILD COULD
PASS AS A HUMAN BEING. AT NO TIME, HOWEVER, DID
MR. J.G.O. ADMIT THAT HE WAS THE INFANT'S FATHER.
"IT'S NOT EASY TO GIVE UP YOUR OWN CALF,"
JULIA SOBBED. "BUT THIS CALF NEEDS A MOMMY AND
DADDY TO RAISE HIM. HE HAS A WONDERFUL PERSON-
ALITY COMBINING THE BRAVERY OF A BULL WITH THE
PLACIDITY OF A COW. HE'S ALWAYS MOOING, AND I
JUST KNOW HE'LL MAKE SOME LUCKY COUPLE VERY
HAPPY AND GIVE THEM A LOT OF LOVE. OF COURSE, IF
THEY HAD A LOVELY GRASSY FIELD BEHIND THIER
HOUSE, IT WOULD MAKE ME VERY HAPPY, SINCE I'D
NEED A PLACE TO GRAZE WHEN I VISIT."
IN ALL CONFIDENTIALITY, JULIA REVEALED TO A
CLOSE FRIEND THAT IF SHE EVER EXPOSED MR. J.G.O. AS
BEING THE FATHER OF HER CHILD, HE WOULD NOT
HESITATE TO MAKE HAMBURGER MEAT OUT OF HER.

"What do the tea leaves say? Is the time propitious for me
to tell him to go to hell?" I ask Kathy.
"You don't have to be that tough on him; after all he's

in Brazil, not around the corner."
"So should I write him a letter?" Juvenal no longer exists
for me. I resent his persistence. Once I'm done with a project,
I'm done with it.
"I wouldn't."
"No?" I'm relieved.
"Unless you want to. Do you want to?"
"I'm kind of curious about how he's going to end the
complete and unexpurgated Memoirs of a Rakehell from
Brazil."
"Wanna bet he goes on and on, never ending, like a
shaggy bitch story?" Kathy likes saying bitch. She doesn't have
to be politically correct around me. All she has to be is funny.
"Some men who have a macho attitude still think
that if a woman's an artist she's also a whore—or a mother
confessor," Kathy says. "This guy thinks you're both."
"Naw, he respects me. We discussed a movie together.
He confided in me."
"Men confide in women they don't know as easily as
they fuck women they don't know. They think it's their
birthright."
"S'funny, I think it's my birthright too," I say.

13

YOUR FEET ARE THE GATEWAY TO YOUR SOUL

A man I once knew was fixated on my feet. He loved to kiss and caress them, to suck my big toe, to lick between each little pink piggy, to have me walk on him. For these stolen moments (he was married to a woman who refused to satisfy his cravings) he'd wear a special velvet jacket which was soft and thick and gave off little sparks of electricity as I traversed him. His fascination, at first an innocent diversion that gave him great joy, became his downfall since (punishment from heaven?) he managed to catch a disease that resembled foot-fungus on his tongue. A skin specialist advised him to give up his obsessive behavior before it killed him. (This is what he told me before we broke up) All I can say is, he didn't get it from me since I've never had a skin disease anywhere on my body. I am reminded of Bunuel's *L'Age D'Or*: the garden scene where a woman sucks the big toe of a naked male statue. It really doesn't matter what one puts into ones mouth, it always looks pornographic.

artfab@mama.ed

LOUISE BOURGEOIS IS THE FIRST SCULPTOR TO HAVE CARVED BUNIONS IN MARBLE. ONE COMES UPON THEM BY SURPRISE AFTER HAVING OBSERVED THE REST OF THE CARVING: A WELL FORMED FEMALE IN TRADITIONAL SEMI-RECLINING POSE. SLYLY, THERE ARE THE FEET! AND ONE IMAGINES THE SOUR-LEMON SMILE OF BOURGEOIS HERSELF. THE BONE GROWS OUTWARD: A PAINFUL GROTESQUERY. A RUDE REMINDER OF THE WAY THINGS

ARE. THIS SCULPTURAL MALFORMATION IS BOURGEOIS' COMMENT ON THE SENTIMENTALITY AND FALSE PERFECTION OF RODIN'S STATUES OF NAKED WOMEN WHICH FIND THEIR PARALLEL IN THOSE AIR BRUSHED PHOTOGRAPHS SEEN IN PLAYBOY AND OTHER MAGAZINES.
Nana here. Ugh! Take it away. I like pretty pictures. Turner seascapes. Blakelock trees. The tarry boats and thick lemon moons of Ryder.
SO WHAT. I LIKE IDA APPLEBROOG, CAN'T GET ANY PRETTIER THAN THAT. THE STAGE IS SET. THE PLAYERS STRUCK DUMB. THE HUMAN COMEDY ADVANCES IN SILENCE. WHEN THE TITLES APPEAR, FEAR TAKES ALL THE CREDIT.
You really like her?
YEAH.
Better than who? Daumier? Munch?
MUNCH? YOU MEAN BECAUSE OF THE SILENT SCREAM? NAH. AND DAUMIER REVEALED THE CORRUPTION OF PUBLIC OFFICIALS, ETC. HE WAS COOL, CLEVER, AND FUNNY. NOT AN ARTIST OF THE SCREAM, SILENT OR OTHERWISE. APPLEBROOG IS A TERRIFIC FEMINIST/HUMANIST/ARTIST. AS LONG AS INJUSTICE AND CRUELTY EXIST IN THE HOME, OFFICE, AND SEEDY HOTEL ROOMS, SHE WILL SEEK IT OUT AND SHOW IT FOR WHAT IT IS.
Brava! Do you know her?
NO.

14

"Josef is suffering in prison," Marie says. "The food's too salty and the population is hostile—He misses you, Julia." She reapplies her lipstick, pats her hair into place. "Nice place you have," she says. "Josef would be happy here."

"I thought he'd get out on bail; how come he's still in prison?" I am taping Marie. She is at her self-conscious best.

"They don't trust him. I myself asked him whether he'd go on the lam if he got out on bail, and he said he would. He's my son but I'll never understand him." She takes a snapshot of him out of her handbag; holds it up for the camera. "He's eleven years old here, riding his first horse. See how proud he is? A friend of his happened to take this picture just before he fell off the horse. There was some barbed wire in the field and he cut his knee on it. It was a deep cut. I wasn't with him when it happened. The camp director told me that he didn't cry when they stitched it up. Before he went off to camp he'd had a tetanus shot. Pure luck. You never know do you." She kisses the photo before sliding it back into her purse.

"What does he mean by, 'the population is hostile'?"

"He's received death threats."

"Then they should isolate him from the other prisoners."

"They don't give a damn about him. The guards call him The Mad Scientist."

"Why?"

"Because he heals skin lesions by pressing onion slices to them, lances boils with toothpicks, that sort of thing. He should be in a mental ward according to the prison psychologist."

"Does he ask after me?"

87

"He doesn't understand why you're so frightened of him."

"I might visit him. Think that's a good idea?"

"He'd be overjoyed. However, I don't think he'll be in jail much longer."

"No?"

"His attorney says that Josef didn't kill Dwayne, and that there is evidence that Dwayne died of congenital heart disease."

"Can he prove it?"

SEPARATED BY BULLETPROOF GLASS

I can't touch Josef: we are separated by a thick pane of glass. Sound is transmitted through a chrome microphone set into the window. There are many visitors today stretching the length of the room, leaning forward, arms on the small ledge in front of them: some are whispering (not wanting to be overheard by the guards), others (incautiously) shout to make sure they are heard. Kisses are given by touching the mouth then pressing the dampened fingers to the glass, or in the case of a few emotionally stressed visitors, pressing the lips directly to the glass (while the prisoner on the other side presses his to exactly the same spot). Josef looks better than I've ever seen him. All of his hair's been shaved off in the prison barber shop, and his face is clean shaven.

"Magotty. Does that describe me, Julia?" he asks.

"Not at all."

"Good. Because I don't have queer notions; I'm not full of whims. I've been reading the dictionary. There are so many words to consider. At first I was afraid I was maggoty."

"Not at all. As an example, maggots don't have legs."

"Guess that settles that—thanks for coming," he says. "I don't get many visitors."

"Well I'm still your wife," I say, as if that's the reason for my visit. Does Josef actually believe that marital duty kicks in only when the spouse is incarcerated? Up until now I've done my best to avoid him. He must know that! His face assumes the serious mein of a physician who has bad news. "Is that a blister on your finger?" He tries to take my hand but his knuckles come up hard against the glass partition.

"It's nothing—a small burn; I put some ice on it, but it blistered anyway."

"If it opens put First-Aid Cream on it," he is really concerned. He believes in cause and effect. Injury—neglect—death.

"Thanks, I will."

"There have been attempts made on my life," he whispers, cutting across his throat with a finger. "I'm over qualified for the job."

"What job?"

"Medical adjunct to the chief prison surgeon. Things are topsy-turvy, I should be the chief surgeon. He's put out a contract on my secondary sexual characteristics." He glances around to see if we're being observed.

"Your balls?" I would have liked to say "cojones" but it would have been too dramatic; Josef would have demanded to know where I had heard the word. Up in Washington Heights with a drug dealer? Am I familiar with any other Spanish words? Puta, for instance? "Cojones" could open the floodgates of fear and retaliation: feed Josef's pathological jealousy of me. "Your balls?" I repeat.

"You've got to save them for me. If you happen to receive a refrigerated package from me in the near future, I want you to put it in the freezer and keep it for me. Do not defrost. You understand? Do not defrost! Do not refreeze!"

"Okay—but why don't you send the package to your mother? She's an old hand at food storage."

"Read your Freud," he says seriously, "the part about Oedipus; then substitute testes for eyes."

"Your mom says Dwayne probably dropped dead on his own, had heart disease, so if you're feeling guilty, or have nightmares, stop! You don't have to suffer on Dwayne's account."

"Yeah, bastard got what was coming to him."

"You deserve to have a good life."

"You willing to take me back and sleep with me?"

ALL I WANT TO DO IS CALM THE MAN DOWN, DIRECT HIS THOUGHTS AWAY FROM CASTRATION. I DO NOT WANT TO SLEEP WITH THIS GIGANTIC SLUG-A-BED AGAIN. IT IS NOT LIKE ME TO LIE; IF I TELL HIM I WILL SLEEP WITH HIM THEN I WILL, BUT IF I TELL HIM I WON'T, I MIGHT BE THE ONE RESPONSIBLE FOR DRIVING HIM OVER THE EDGE.

"Marie gave me your address," he continues, "I'm familiar with the place: almost took it once myself. Have a friend used to live there, name of Clov."

I do not betray recognition. "Clov? What an odd name."

"Not so odd: the devil had clov feet, right? Excuse me, cloven hooves." Suddenly tears fill his eyes. He allows them to trail down his cheeks, his neck, and into the collar of his prison issue work shirt; he is unaware that he is crying soundlessly and without emotion.

"What's the devil got to do with Clov?"

"He had two small bumps on his forehead looked just like horns. Made him devilishly weird; he was afraid of going out because of them. But he got lucky. Was only a phone call away from happiness, and didn't know it."

"Who'd he call? God?"

"Modern Hair Weavers."

"He was bald?"

"Partially bald, and partially horned. The man absolutely swears by the technique of hair weaving; now he can go swimming without fear, stand on a windy hill, or run the marathon with complete confidence. Said it changed his life."

"It did?"

"Hair hid his horns. Made him more desirable to the opposite sex and religion."

"The opposite religion?"

"One horn a Unicorn makes, two horns a Jewish person."

"You believe that shit?"

"That's what they believe in Bellingham, Washington where I was brought up. Clov was born there, too; not in Ireland as previously reported."

"Do you know where Clov is now?" I have more than a passing interest in his whereabouts: what if Hamm visits me again, asks if I've heard from Clov?

"To the beach. He said he wanted to breath the clean sea air. Make a pillow of sand for his head."

WHAT IS THERE TO KEEP ME HERE?

"What beach?"

"Didn't specify. Does it matter? A beach is a beach."

"A beach is not a beach," I'm too agitated to argue the point.

"What do you mean Julia? Are you trying to confuse me?"

Bell clangs. Visiting hour is over. Josef rises slowly, "Write to me Julia. I'll wait for your letter before sending that package. I've got to know where I stand with you."

Josef is getting better (saner); I surmise this from purely circumstantial evidence: he did not send me his balls as promised. Instead, I received a paisley skirt ordered by him from L.L. Bean's, and delivered within two days by Federal Express. I intended to wear it on visiting day, show myself off, but instead (finally) Nukler got him out on bail (and I didn't know where to find him)—and then he fired Nukler anyway, accusing him of being a mouthpiece for terrorists and murderers (as if he didn't know that already). I guess he is going to handle his own case: so many nuts do. It might work if the squirrels don't get him first.

HIDEOUT REVEALED

He's in Maine, (his letter arrived today) at the Smithson Laboratory, a laboratory that breeds mice for laboratory research conducted throughout the world. His kind of place. Clov is with him (he says).

"He finds the Maine woods more soothing than the ocean which causes Hepatitis B, Jaundice, diarrhea, and fever with every mouthful. I agree with him," Josef reports, "but I haven't told him about deer ticks yet. We've developed a warm friendship, Clov and I, in this isolated place. And he doesn't mind that I'm a parolee, doesn't guzzle all the apple cider leaving none for me, and the man does whatever I want him to do without complaining, the way you used to do when I was too tired to come to dinner."

AH GREAT FUN, WE HAD, THE TWO OF US, GREAT FUN.

"THERE'S A RAT IN THE KITCHEN!"
"A RAT! ARE THERE STILL RATS?"
I've found more than one empty rat trap in my apartment. At night they continue to sing to one another because Clov is gone.

SOON I WON'T DO IT ANY MORE

Josef has enclosed a clipping from USA Today about Laboratory use of a new gene to genetically engineer mice to mimic the human disease (cystic fibrosis): the scientists have learned that the cystic fibrosis gene acts as a pump in the cells of the lung. Its mutation causes the buildup of lung secretions, a hallmark of the disease. This discovery is leading to possible gene therapy for cystic fibrosis within a year or two. At last Josef is involved in something important, and even if his court case interrupts his research (I'm sure he'll be proven innocent) he'll be able to return to it. He can thank computers for that: whatever he files away will stay there till he gets back.

FALSE CREDENTIALS DO NOT MEAN THAT THE PRESENTER OF SUCH A FRAUDULENT DOCUMENT IS IN-CAPABLE OF DOING A GOOD JOB. I HAVE NO IDEA WHAT

JOSEF TOLD HIS EMPLOYERS AT THE LAB, BUT IT MUST
HAVE BEEN CONVINCING.

**IF CLOV IS HAMM'S TYPE, CAN HE BE
JOSEF'S TOO?**

No.

DOES CLOV EXIST IN THE REAL WORLD?

Who?

15

Drinks at the Met. Expensive drinks. At least I never pay the suggested price of admission: I give 'em five cents. That's all it takes to get in. I could give 'em one cent and they'd have to take it. Artist's should be allowed in free. The metal button (handed out at admission) fits into a buttonhole: tiny tag inserted, then bent back against the material. Seeing this museum button, the guard allows me to pass. I find an unoccupied table above the restaurant to wait at. Jane and Kathy are meeting me. Jane is about to return to the U.K. and Kathy is hot to tell me about a savage incident in Brazil: police killing kids. She's so afraid I'll go there to have an affair with J.G.O. Never in a freaky-deaky million years. America is my trysting place.

"Order me one of those," Kathy says, pointing to my glass of chablis. "It looks so cool. Is it good?"

"Tastes good. No vinegar aftertaste."

"What an expert," she's pretty snotty.

"Who gives a shit about wine?" I say. "Half of France is alcoholic just to support their vineyards and wineries. Can't put a viand into their bouches without swishing a tingly mouthful of anaesthetic around. Pretentious bastards, I'll never speak their language."

"Hey, all I said was—"

"You said, 'What an expert.' Well I'm not in the mood for sardonic humor, okay?"

"Okay—Jane coming?"

"Yes, Jane is coming."

"Say what makes you so lovable today?"

"Nobody loves me, and I don't have anyone to love. I'm out on a papier-mache limb by myself."

"You saw Josef, right? And he bugged you."

"He's out of jail, can move around the planet like an ordinary citizen; and he's working with mice again in a New England lab; keeps calling me to ask the meanings of words. Suddenly he loves words! Has a dictionary, but depends on me to elucidate. If I take too long answering him, he threatens to kill me. The man's still nuts!"

I KANT SAY WHAT KANT BE SAID

"How'd he get out of jail?"

"The coroner's report—Dwayne died of congenital heart failure—I know that millions of people watching the Geraldo Show saw Josef stab Dwayne on the left side of his chest, but life is stranger than fiction."

"How much stranger?"

"Dwayne's heart was on the right side of his body—freak of nature—Josef has Dwayne's misplaced heart to thank for the fact that he's not facing a murder charge."

Kathy crosses herself. "Fan-fucking-tastic!"

"Yeah."

The wine arrives. Kathy imbibes. Inhales. Exhales. Settles back. Jane arrives. She sits. Puts a full plastic shopping bag on the floor between her legs.

"Anything interesting in there?" Kathy asks.

"Things to give as gifts back home. What are you drinking?"

"Expensive white wine." I say.

"How expensive?"

"$4.75 a glass. You can spend more if you want to." I hand her the wine list.

"I'll have some bottled water. Wine makes me sleepy. I'm not ready to go to sleep."

"You never are," I say, "yet you fall asleep at the drop of a hat."

"True, true. Something must be wrong with my metabolism; however, I keep going—Went to the Whitney before I came here. Impressive in a pubic-phobic-conceptual way."

She digs a catalogue out of the bag on the floor, hands it to me. "Made me sick especially a kind of spidery sculpture constructed of 6 foot dreadlocks! The thing was made of real hair swept up from the floor of a barber shop. Truly disgusting. I'd hate to see any part of my body swept up and exhibited on a museum floor."

"You're not an artist," I say. "The more disgusting an artist is, the better he or she likes it. That pussy freak Annie Sprinkle for instance. Her claim to fame—urinating on stage."

ART DOES (NOT!) EXIST

The waiter brings Jane her Perrier in its cold, sweaty green bottle. She pours it nicely, holding it at a distance from the glass so that it splashes. "I could take a shower in this stuff," she admits.

Kathy says, "I love an English accent."

"You said you have something to tell me about Brazil," I remind her, "out with it."

She puts a page she has pulled from a magazine on the table. "Read it and weep," she says.

MR. J.G.O. CONFESSES HE IS A VAMPIRE
I KILLED TWENTY GIRLS TO DRINK THEIR BLOOD
WHILE IT WAS STILL HOT

A brutal serial killer raped and murdered twenty young girls, then drank their blood from a Waterford crystal champagne glass. When asked why he did this gruesome thing, he replied matter of factly: "Because, this cocktail is the fountain of youth! Who wouldn't drink from it? It's put the sparkle back in my eyes, the bounce into my step, and the steel into my prick."

The vampire, identified as Mr. J.G.O., president of a steel company, confessed today after he was arrested by police in Rio de Janeiro, Brazil, authorities say. When apprehended he put up no resistance and seemed eager to answer the questions put to him. His victims, all girls between the ages of ten to fifteen and from the slums, were offered money to come with him to church, and to light candles for him. None ever made it to church—or home again. The bloodthirsty monster would take these trusting girls to an isolated area where he sexually assaulted them. He would then strangle the girls and dump their bodies along the roadway like hunks of rotting trash.

"I only drank their blood if they were pretty and had a spark of life in their eyes," J.G.O. told police. "I knew that if I drank their blood I would live forever."

"The killer feels no remorse since he is a religious man and believes that the innocent children went straight to heaven," a policeman said.

MORE NEWS FROM BRAZIL!
POLICE HUNT HOMELESS BOYS WHO SLEEP IN THE SHADOWS OF THE CITY'S SYMBOLS OF LUXURY AND POWER ITS MUSEUMS, HOTELS, AND MUNICIPAL BUILDINGS

"Only poor kids are killed," Jane says. "The children of the rich don't sleep in the streets."

"I'm going to write Juvenal a letter ending our correspondence," I say. "Affluent bastard! He should be targeted for death, not homeless children."

Jane tries to calm me down. "My dear, dear Julia, you are doing a video installation based on an interview with the man; now you have more material to work with—it's marvelous luck! I'd continue to write to him."

16

IT AIN'T EASY FINDIN' REAL FREAK ACTS
THESE DAYS!!

"My sister," Stan Baltimore says, "would like to meet you. She's never met a real artist."

"I'm just like anyone else."

"No you're not."

"Yes, I am."

"Believe me Julia, there's a big difference."

"Like what?"

"You think everyone is interesting. You don't believe in evil. And your brassiere is full of quarters."

"How do you know?"

"Saw it hanging in the closet. It was heavy."

"Yeah? Well how much money do I have?"

"Sixteen dollars in quarters."

"You counted?"

"How come you don't wear a brassiere? Your tits are heavier than sixteen dollars in quarters. I'd like to weigh them."

"Asshole. I'm gonna be late with the rent this month. Weigh that!"

"You still fuckin' that Brazilian billionaire?"

"Whatdya mean?"

"Saw him around the corner in the bodega."

"Must've been a look alike."

"His car and chauffeur were waiting for him."

"He's in Rio de Janeiro. Just got a letter from him."

"Hot stuff! I read it."

"Hey why don't you get off my case?"

"I'm in love with you. I want you to meet my sister."

"I could have you arrested for harassing me."

"You wouldn't do that."

"No?"

"You're trying to keep a low profile, so the law'll forget about you."

"Look Stan, you think you've got the goods on me but you're living in Sueno land: I haven't fucked any billionaires, I'm not married to a murderer, and the law doesn't have anything on me."

"You're a bitch on wheels Ms. Maraini; I love it!"

"Do you mind telling me how you got into my apartment again? There's a new lock on the door, so I..."

"Who says I came in the door?"

"Didn't you?"

"I came in through the bathroom window."

"There is no bathroom window."

"Look again...It was boarded up."

"That's breaking and entering."

"There was an emergency: water leak."

"What does it take to get you off my back?"

"Meet my sister. She's a swell person. It'll only take a few minutes of your time."

"Okay."

"You might want to make a video of her...she's kind of different."

"How different?"

"You'll see."

17

Juan and I are downing some brew. It's Saturday; early evening. He's here because he's lonely, and to let me know that a piece of his is in the Latin American Artists of the Twentieth Century show at MoMA.

"I had the best time on that mattress before I burned it and hung it on the wall," he says. "Frank loves that piece."

"Have you heard from him?"

"Twice a day. He's in Provincetown now, smelling leather and eating silver rivets at the A House small bar; Frank's too sexy for his own good."

"I thought he was in Seattle."

"He never stays long in one place."

"No?"

"Says he bought me a piano to destroy. Miss Thing is so stupid. I don't know how many times I've told him I don't do that anymore. It's as if I was Yoko Ono and he expected me to make the fly movie again, or climb into a bag and wait for people to kick me. Whatever. Sometimes I think it's intentional. How can anyone be that dumb."

"When's he coming back?"

"Tomorrow, next week, who cares!"

LIFE GOES ON

"You know that you care darling."

"Enough about me. What about you?"

"My landlord's been spying on me."

"Is he cute?"

"Come on Juan! He could be dangerous."

"Want me to scare the living daylights out of him?"

"How?"

"The usual way. I'll tell him I want him, and he'll drop dead on the spot."

"He's bringing his sister to meet me. It's very odd to say the least."

"Odd things always happen to you Julia; you're famous for it. Oddballs gravitate toward you knowing they have come to the right place. You of course have heard that Dick Gull (The Guy) was arrested by a pair of short detectives in Hawaiian shirts before he could make his getaway to Rio?"

"He's innocent."

"Of course he's innocent."

"He's protecting someone."

"I know."

"You do?"

"Yes my dear—Dick is madly in love with me—he's protecting me. It was I who started that fire. A total accident I swear to you! I was in this filthy, empty lot next to the rug store, setting fire to a half-dozen, twin size, Sealy innerspring mattresses that I'd bought on the cheap from Salvation Army, when suddenly a wind came up and blew the flames in the direction of the store. There was nothing I could do about it Julia, nothing at all. But I needed those mattresses; you should see them: they're so wonderful, the springs exposed and twisted, the stuffing bursting through; most of the original stains are still there—my best work—so when the coast was clear a few days later I returned with my truck to pick them up."

"Why haven't you told the investigators?"

"And waste the publicity! I'm saving my confession to coincide with the opening of my retrospective next month— By the way, has *People Magazine* called you?"

"Apropos of what?"

"To do a story on you and Josef. I've heard rumors."

"Think I should?"

"You're asking me? My dear I'd sell my fingerprints to the highest bidder."

"They'll want to take pictures of us—Josef isn't here.

This is not our cozy little love nest."

"Where is he?"

"In Maine with (I whisper) Clov."

"Clov? Is he taking a course in cooking?"

"He's having an affair with a man—a famous character."

"Well this is a new development! Next thing you'll be telling me you're shacking up with Kathy."

"Don't hold your breath."

"You don't convince me Miss Pure! I've seen you two together."

"Thanks Juan, for trying to insert a little fictive excitement into my life, but it won't work—my frail barque has been tossed upon the dinner salad of life once too often."

"That's beautiful, about the 'frail barque'..."

"Thanks."

18

Here I sit in this box of a kitchen (my world and the world Clov wants to return to, according to last night's dream, in which he appeared to me). In this world/kitchen I shield myself from those two terrorists (my parents) who no longer exist, but who find me anyway. In their defense, they did not set out to terrorize me: they were simply living their own unhappy lives—and using their experience (limited as it was) to give advice and to make decisions concerning me. I have only compassion for them now, though I can still hear him cursing her, and can see her alone, carefully packing household objects, wrapping dishes in newspaper before putting them into wooden barrels. "You're never here to help me," she says to him.

THE UNANSWERED QUESTION: "WHY DID LOVE FAIL?"

Years later, told to me in confidence, she'd said: "He put a girlie magazine over my face so he could do 'you know what' to me."

DO CHILDREN HAVE TO KNOW THESE THINGS?

When the screaming began I'd crawl into the box (the one the new refrigerator came in).

When the screaming continued I'd crawl out of my box to bang on their bedroom door, begging them to stop.

When the screaming got louder I drew delicate crisscrosses over the backs of my hands with a razor, blotting the blood with a Kleenex, then, the next day I'd apply "skin color" makeup to the cuts.

Did I have the right to suffer? Wasn't it presumptuous of me to demand attention in the midst of this maelstrom? Should I have taken their misfortunes to heart, as I did? And when I interview my subjects, digging deep (with the razor of intellect, pretending art is a game), am I searching for myself?

WHAT SELF FOR GOD'S SAKE?

Q: What self?

A: The shelf life of a self depends on whether you can keep moving, sell yourself to others. There are many selves fighting for the space you occupy. Some of these selves have better representation than you have: influential people who back them up, exaggerate their capabilities, lend them money, answer urgent messages.

Q: Who represents you?

A: Those who are either dead or powerless.

Q: That's the way it goes.

A: I let it go that way. NOT HAVING increases one's desire to have. Meanwhile I'm changing. I'm ready for something good to happen to me.

Q: Like what?

A: A grant so that I can continue my work; enough money is one way to avert a crisis. (FOOLING MYSELF AGAIN?)

I SAY TO MYSELF—JULIA YOU MUST LEARN TO SUFFER BETTER THAN THAT IF YOU WANT THEM TO WEARY OF REWARDING OTHERS.

PAID ADVERTISEMENT

IF YOU'VE BEEN UNSURE ABOUT JOINING JULIA MARAINI'S HAVE-A-KISS-CLUB, WHY NOT ORDER HER NEW PLAY GUIDE FOR SINGLES.

SHE'S WRITTEN THIS PLAYLET FOR THOSE OF YOU WHO MAY WANT SOME SIMPLE ADVICE ON HOW TO:

PREPARE A KISS REQUEST, OR REPLY TO ONE, PUT FORWARD YOUR BEST IDEAS ON KISSING, OVERCOME NERVOUS JITTERS DURING THAT SECOND OR THIRD KISS, AND MANY MORE HELPFUL HINTS. DON'T LET YOUR UNCERTAINTY KEEP YOU FROM WHAT COULD BE A REWARDING EXPERIENCE. MEASURING TAPES IN BLUE OR YELLOW LAMINATED COTTON CAN BE PURCHASED (FOR USE WHEN SOMEONE TELLS YOU TO KEEP YOUR DISTANCE) BY SENDING $2.50 TO JULIA MARAINI (MEASURING TAPES), BOX 64, NYC, NY 10012. THE PLAY GUIDE CAN ALSO BE PURCHASED, SAME ADDRESS, FOR AN ADDITIONAL $4.00.

Continued on next page.

HAVE-A-KISS-CLUB

Play Guide #1
KRAPP'S NEXT TO LAST TAPE
"Kiss me (pause) Will you not kiss me?"
"No."
"On the cheek?"
"You're too far away."
"Five inches away."
"Miles away."
"The tape says five inches."
"The tape is too literal."
"Do you think I'm too ugly to be kissed?"
"I won't dignify that with an answer."
"I've degraded myself with a question."
"Look in the mirror. Mirrors never lie."
"I'm glad you won't kiss me. The last time I had to wipe spittle from my cheek."
"You didn't tell me."
"Didn't want to hurt your feelings."
"And now?"
"I want to."

"Okay I'll kiss you."
"Darling."
"Darling."

19

STAN AND HIS SISTER, THAT DANCING DUO, INVADE MY STUDIO AND SHOCK THE SHIT OUT OF ME

At first I hear a drum being beaten. Street musician? No. It's right outside my door. Next I hear sharp metallic tapping to a once popular tune: East Side, West Side (All Around the Town)—Sounds very professional to me—Could be some lost tap dancers who have wandered away from their own kind: those who congregate in front of Macy's department store once a year (whether it's cloudy or sunny) to dance for the public in the midst of a mob.

"Who is it?"

No reply. The beat goes on. I fling the door open.

"SURPRISE! It's us."

Stan Baltimore and his sister, both in tap shoes: she wearing a veil over her face, he in a top hat, push their way past me into the living room.

"Jazz is all," Stan says, "but tapping to jazz is the jazziest thing in the world."

"Ditto," his sister says.

"May I take your veil?" I ask politely. "I'll put it in the closet for you."

She cringes.

"She never takes her veil off," Stan says, "She's a woman of mystery."

"Hell, it's just me." I say.

"Not for anyone," Stan says. "Listen to this." He fast forwards the tape on the microrecorder he's holding to "Let Yourself Go." He sings a few bars: "Come get together/Let the dance floor feel your leather/ dance as lightly as a

feather/Let yourself go."
    I can tell he's not sure of the words. He repeats the same stanza over again. "I prefer the instrumental version," I say. "To each his own," he replies. "How about this?" He plays "Puttin' On The Ritz."
    His sister taps her heart out in short order. He taps a circle around her. They bow. I try to see under her veil. Nothing. For all I know she has no face. Could be a war casualty. A crash victim. Someone who's just had a bad face lift and recent dermabrasion. Juan says I'm an outpost for oddballs. He's right. I'm a magnet. Mother Theresa is a magnet. Lots of swell people are magnets. Something to do with energy arrows all pointing in the same direction that attract other energy arrows pointing in the same direction (or is it in the opposite direction?). Math and science have never been a strong point with me—Yeah, I'm curious, but not curious enough to spend my life researching the subject—What makes the world go 'round?—Joel Grey in *Cabaret* said that money makes the world go round—My opinion? Greed makes the world go 'round. Once I thought I knew what gravity was/does, that it kept us safely anchored to earth—now I know different—sentimental attachments keep us here.
    Dance ends. The Baltimore sister collapses into the wheelchair (my favorite stage for those I interview). She is breathing hard. Stan rushes to the kitchen for a glass of water. He brings one back for his sister. He stands in front of her blocking my view as he lifts her veil to give her a drink.
    They consult with each other in hushed tones.
    He lets her veil fall back into place.
    "She likes you," he says. "She'll talk to you."

A STRICTLY SECRET TALK BETWEEN NOTION BALTIMORE AND JULIA MARAINI

J.M. My name is Julia, what is yours?
N.B. (muffled sound) Notion.

J.M. Louder please.

N.B. NOTION!

J.M. Unusual name—do you mind explaining?

N.B. My mother used to listen to Lady Day sing that song: Aint Nobody's Business But My Own—She really dug it, especially the part, If I take a NOTION to jump into the ocean, ain't nobody's business but my own. She grooved on the idea of NOTION. It was like a notion meant you could take your own life if you wanted to. I mean she had this NOTION that love meant you'd be willing to kill yourself for someone. Scared me, cause I thought my momma was going to let me drown in the ocean. Never got over my fear of water.

LET'S GO FROM HERE, THE TWO OF US!...I'LL MAKE A RAFT AND THE CURRENTS WILL CARRY US AWAY, FAR AWAY, TO OTHER...MAMMALS!

J.M. And your second name? Is that Baltimore?

N.B. Same as my brother's. I was born in Baltimore, on the waterfront, whilst momma was waitin' for a fried clam dinner to arrive. I was a beautiful baby.

J.M. Your face was...?

N.B. Beautiful.

J.M. Then why do you hide it behind a veil? Veils are no longer worn.

N.B. Do you happen to have a pain killer around? My head's too heavy to hold up without a pain killer, and I've used mine up.

J.M. The only thing I have is a few old Percodan's.

N.B. Anything! Jerry Lewis, used to be addicted to Percodan's, did you know that?

J.M. Who's Jerry Lewis?—Hey, here, try these. I put two tablets into her hand.

AT THE MOMENT NOTHING MUCH IS HAPPENING. WE ARE JOCKEYING FOR POSITION. WHAT PASSES FOR TRUTH IS NOT. THERE IS NOTHING NATURAL ABOUT AN

INTERVIEW. NOTION SEEMS TO BE SLIDING DOWN THE CHAIR. STAN LIFTS HER BACK INTO AN UPRIGHT POSITION. HE PUTS HIMSELF BESIDE HER CHAIR TO PHOTOGRAPH ME WITH HIS CAMERA. SOON (WHEN HIS FILM IS DEVELOPED) IT WILL BE POSSIBLE FOR THE MUSEUM CROWD TO OBSERVE ME "PAINTING" MY SUBJECT, WHILE WATCHING MYSELF IN THE MIRROR BEHIND STAN BALTIMORE: MARAINI(!) A VELASQUEZ FOR THE NINETIES! LAS MENINAS LIVES!

N.B. I once had everything: lovers, money, fame. Everyone envied me. Now when people see me they get sick. My face—it's horribly changed.

J.M. (Becoming concerned) Are you a fire victim? Were you scarred? (Could she have been in my old building when it burned?)

N.B. Worse. My life was turned upside down when I suddenly contracted neurofibromatosis—Elephant Man's disease. The Elephant Man, he got the best of it: the jobs, money, love. A movie about him! Okay so it was sad when he couldn't lift his head off the pillow and choked to death. Same thing might happen to me, but I don't have a cent to show for it!

J.M. You don't?

N.B. My husband stole all of my credit cards, emptied my bank account, and kicked me out. I had to beg outside of Penn Station to get enough to eat. I was too embarrassed to ask Stan for help. However, he found me, and here I am on my feet again—well barely.

J.M. Can't anything be done, medically?

N.B. My lovely face is now a grotesque mask of dangling skin folds and tumors. You may have seen the article in SUN of a similar case. We have an international organization that raises money for research—so far no consequential discoveries.

J.M.　How about plastic surgery?

N.B.　Temporary relief.The growths would come back. Hey it's okay. I'm blind. I have a great brother, and friends on the street. What's life about anyway? even learned to tap! Who would have expected that? If I die, this interview will bear witness that I was here. Do you want to see my face? I think it should be on the video. Yes, it should be. So what if it makes people violently ill!

J.M.　Don't say that: not everybody would have that strong a reaction to you. Did you happen to see that movie with Cher in it, called "Mask"? She had a son who had your disease, and she loved him, and he was a great guy. In fact I think you have a good chance of entering the mainstream if you stay with it, stay with life I mean. There's a celebrity somewhere I'm sure, who would be happy to rally to your cause.

N.B.　(Shouting) They're all taken: they rally round the biggies: cancer, HIV, Lou Gehrig's Disease!

J.M.　I think Robert DeNiro's free. Maybe you could get him.

N.B.　Sure! If I send him a tape of me singin' "Don't Explain."

DO YOU KNOW WHAT'S HAPPENED?
IT HAPPENED TO ME BUT I WASN'T THERE.
DO YOU KNOW WHEN IT HAPPENED?
I DON'T KNOW. THINGS JUST TAKE THEIR COURSE.

　　She removes her veil. I gasp. Her face is—lovely(!): perfectly smooth, symmetrical, untroubled. If there is disease it has not manifested itself in the flesh.
　　Stan catches me as I faint.

　　When I regain consciousness the two detectives are beside me. Mr. Flamingo is rubbing my wrists, Mr. Palm Trees is cradling my head. Noone else is in the room.

"Run away." Detective Flamingo says.

"Where should I go?" This is the advice I've been waiting for.

"How about 72nd Street," Detective Palm Trees says.

"You crazy?" Detective Flamingo says. "It's a melting pot up there."

"Well, where do you recommend I go?" I'm speaking to both of them at once. They bounce up and down with excitement.

Detective Flamingo pulls me toward the TV.

"It's on the Travel Channel," he says. "They work hand in glove with us. We have witnesses stashed all over the globe. You name a hotel, we got a witness or two staying there. Any country you prefer?"

"The U.S.A." I say.

"You fool!" Detective Palm Trees says. "They'll find you here."

"Who'll find me here?"

"That's for us to know and you to find out," Palm Trees and Flamingo do a little dance around me.

"What's this all about?" I sit on the floor, letting them circle me.

"Witness protection, kid. Can't have you knocked off before we get the goods on you," Palm Trees removes a cellophane wrapped toothpick from his shirt pocket. "How'd you like a toothpick. It's mint flavored."

I accept the toothpick. It might come in handy if I have to fight my way out of here.

"Thanks...May I ask you a question?"

"Shoot," Palm Trees says.

"Where?" Detective Flamingo gasps, swiftly ducking into the closet.

"You see how sensitive he is?" Detective Palm Trees says, "he trembles at the least hint of violence, but his shrink won't let him resign until he conquers his fear, or dies of it, whichever comes first."

Coming out of the closet,"Well then, what is your question young lady?"

"Am I being charged with anything?"

"Of course not!" they say, in unison. "You are now in the capable hands of the Witness Protection Division of the Bureau of Criminal Investigation."

"TIME TO TAKE INVENTORY!" Detective Palm Trees shouts.

"You sit there in that wheelchair," Detective Flamingo orders, "Or I'll be forced to hobble your gait with a charming pair of ankle garters," his last threat whispered into my ear so softly, that Detective Palm Trees can't hear him.

The detectives paste a search warrant to my forehead before they search the apartment: "Do not be alarmed," Detective Flamingo says, "this is not happening."

THEY TAKE INVENTORY

At the cupboard: Not even a bone.

Two ashbins: Empty! Except for shallow layer of sand at bottom.

One poster of Jane Avril: torn, poor girl in mid-dance.

Small stepladder: Unsteady, splintery, made of unpainted wood. A household hazard.

One whistle: Made of metal, shrill of sound, a burbling wooden ball bobbing within.

One alarm clock: it's alarm control stuck in the off position, slowly ticking away, its ordinary face turned to the wall.

A telescope: glass dirty, body rusted—stuck in the extended position. What is there to see so far away (?) with only one eye pressed (to it) that is bound to blur.

A rat: liquified in pan below sink, its stench misidentified as "waste matter in old pipes."

The three legged dog: Lame. Deaf. No longer able to hear love's old sweet song.

One sheet: to hang over the windows before filming:

THE END.
They leave quietly, having put the three-legged dog into a bag; taking it with them for evidence. I'll miss it. I identify (unfortunately) with cripples: three-legged dogs, birds caught in tar, baby seals lying bloodied on pure white icefloes, etc.

NOBODY GETS THE ATTENTION THEY NEED. THE EMERGENCY WARDS ARE FULL OF THOSE DYING OF THEIR WOUNDS.

20

Dear Juvenal,

I don't know whether you are in Rio, receiving this letter, or somewhere in the USA incognito, hiding from the law. If you are here (a friend of mine thinks he saw you in my area) and this letter is forwarded to you, please get in touch. I have been reading about you (is it true?) and what you've been up to in your country. It isn't nice! In fact it's revoltingly Sci-fi right down to your horny toes: skin-shedding, blood drinking, kidnappings, and blood curdling shrieks in the night. Say it ain't so. How many lives does a wealthy man have to live in order to prove to himself that he's alive?

Look, I think you should see this great tape I made of you. It's a masterpiece. You might want to buy it from me (yeah, it's pretty incriminating), and I could use the money. I not only could use the money, I NEEEEED it. As far as the next installment of the sexy story you're dying to tell me, I will not read it unless you send me, immediately, a money order for twenty million dollars. You might ask how I arrived at that sum; well, I read it in the papers (a viable extortion sum) and it seems pretty glamorous to me: however, I'm open to negotiation.

Hoping to hear from you pronto by express air mail.

Sincerely yours,
J.M.

21

THE BEST LAID PLANS

Kathy is incredulous: "You did something illegal. Are you trying to get yourself arrested?"

"He'll come up with the money, just you wait and see."

"Only fools think they can get away with this sort of thing."

"I don't think I'll get away with it."

"Are you absolutely, certifiably nuts?"

"Crazy like a fox."

"Now you've got my attention."

"Good...Cause I want him to make the next move. I need something wild to happen in order to finish the J.G.O. project. I could leave it as it is, but what is missing, is..."

"What?"

"The devious, nasty, cruel element of surprise."

LETTERS THAT PASS IN THE NIGHT

Dear Julia,

I hope you are well, and hard at work on your videos, but that you find time to think of me now and then. I have taken a small vacation from family and friends, and find myself in a small, exclusive resort off the coast of Brazil where I will not be disturbed by anyone. Nobody but you knows that I am here.

Should you be asked, please do not divulge my where-abouts. And most important DO NOT BELIEVE ANYTHING ANYONE TELLS YOU ABOUT ME! I have not committed a crime. I am not a monster. I am not maluco! I am an ordinary man who speaks many languages but prefers his own.

I know that you have been wondering what happened to those two lovers (myself and my delicious daughter-in-law) whose exciting tale I began in my last letter...well, wonder no more...

We had to interrupt our pleasure to partake of lunch: I in the main dining room, served on gold rimmed plates, and she with my son in their sitting room, taking advantage of the sultry afternoon to make love after lunch. As I ate the sweet lobster tail set before me, I could hear her cries of pleasure from the room above: Ah! Oh! Ah! This pleasurable sound continued through coffee and dessert (a rich eggy flan covered with caramel sauce) driving me mad with desire, however a merciful silence had ensued by the time I lighted my cigar, and my son (dutiful as always) descended the stairs to accompany my wife to the city on some small errand. Taking advantage of this opportunity to continue our earlier dalliance, I entered my daughter-in-law's apartment. Amused, though God knows why, at the erect state of my prick, she ordered me to "Come here; let me sponge you off."

There was a washbasin beside the bed; as she began to wash me, my tool became even bigger than before. I took it firmly in hand and (lifting her to me) pushed it easily into her cunt, which was still wet with sperm.

She broke out laughing with pleasure (not derision, thank God), and pretended to resist. In this way we fell to the bed, merrily, whereupon making haste I lifted her dress and laid bare her cunt (described in my previous letter). If I have said before that she was as tan and soft as calf's leather, forget it; her skin was white as milk, and soft as silk—the poetry of her face as fine as Rilke. Strange that I hadn't noticed at first, but the vixen was wearing pretty black stockings embroidered with vertical red clocks, and her calves appeared to be as firm and rounded as her breasts. I topped her friendly hugeness, forcing my prick between her thighs, easing it ever so deliciously into her cunt. When I withdrew, thinking to tease her she jumped up pushed me into a chair beside the bed and topped me, imprisoning my member (Oh willing

117

prisoner!) in her cunt.

She grabbed the back of the chair to balance herself as she rocked back and forth. At each stroke (Where did I get the strength?) her labia touched my balls, warming and embracing them briefly, I imagined that I was listening to the sound of gentle waves lapping against rock. And as I played with her tits she begged me to suck on them, because "It feels so good," she said.

Her nipples were hard and small, larger than my wife's though, and she had some blond hairs growing from their aureolas (a sight that might have disgusted me had I seen them in other circumstances). She was very excited, approaching climax! So violent were her movements that my prick twice slid out of her cunt; I'd been sent from paradise, left to fend for myself (briefly), till she put it back in (too roughly for my taste), enjoying herself at my expense.

"How good your prick feels!" she said, then "Ah! Ah! I'm coming!" As she climaxed, the refined, caring, sweet daughter-in-law bit my shoulder. My tail was hot as hell, I was on the point of discharging when she stood up abruptly, seized my sticky member in her right hand, and began to stroke it, saying—

Unfortunately, just at this moment, my wife and son have returned with their purchases. So, for the time being, you will have to imagine the rest, dear Julia. I will not be able to send you another installment till after I have returned to Rio. Please feel free to write to me. I'm sure you must have stories to tell, you a woman of the world! How nice it is to speak to one who understands the soul of man.

Sincerely yours,

P.S. I know you have never been to Brazil, but have you been to Oahu? Kuaii? Mauii?

YES, TO OAHU, AS A CHILD

OAHU. THE KAHALA HILTON. ORCHIDS ON THE PILLOWS.

Rosalyn Drexler

DOLPHINS IN THE WATERWAY. SUNDAY FOOTBALL GAME. ANNOUNCEMENT INTERRUPTS. JOHN LENNON HAS BEEN KILLED.

22

"Brought your mail up," Jane says.

"Thanks."

"Here's another letter from your Brazilian admirer."

"He must have received my demand for money."

"You brave enough to read his reply?"

"I'll leave it on the table for a while."

"I'd like to know what he says."

"None of your business."

"You know everything about me."

"That's different. It's not personal. Your life is merely my material. I could give a fuck about your actual life as you live it."

"Aren't we being nasty. Don't you love me anymore?"

"Look Jane, it's you made yourself scarce after the interview. I figured you just couldn't face me, so I didn't force things. However I didn't ask you to leave—And I—hey I really dig you—wouldn't mind having you as a roommate if you stayed in New York."

"Bull!...So you going to open the letter?"

"What if Juvenal thinks I'm serious about my demands?"

"Aren't you?"

"And hires some Brazilian hitmen to wipe me out?

"Too late to worry now...Open the damn letter!"

I'm strong enough to resist opening the letter. I take color photos of it as it lies on the table. (Decide to take the camera with me.) How enigmatic an unopened letter is.

We go out to dinner at that Kosher Chinese-Vegetarian place uptown where meat, chicken, and fish are made of soy beans. Juan and Kathy join us, though Kathy prefers real meat.

She hasn't made the connection yet: that meat has to be dead before it can be prepared. She has a new, secret boyfriend that she's keeping under wraps because she doesn't like the way he dresses. She is extremely dress specific about her dates, they have to look German, or Italian...that's because she can't imagine what a Japanese gentleman would wear, and she prefers silk kimonos on her own body, rather than theirs. Maybe she doesn't have a boyfriend.

"I was playing dominoes in the park with a guy says he knows you," she says.

"Yeah?"

"Yeah. He was wearing a short-sleeved black shirt with pink flamingoes on it. Sort of Hawaiian."

"Was he with anyone?"

"Yeah, me."

"Anyone else?"

"Smoke."

"What?"

"The usual salespeople selling smoke; your typical hang. Couldn't tell if they knew him or if he knew them."

"Then why did you mention them?"

"I dunno. I just mentioned them."

"Read your menu, please!"

Ann starts with sweet and sour soup.

Juan has vegetarian won-ton soup.

I skip soup and go right to the fried spring roll.

Kathy orders the appetizer of cold tofu with ginger sauce and chopped scallion.

Juan announces an unexpected visitor: Frank. He's home from P-Town. The waiter brings an extra chair for him. Since he is the food expert, he takes over, decides on, and orders, everyone's main course. He has flair, I decide, ordering the meal in Yiddish with a touch of Chinese sing-song. "Where you learn this?" the waiter asks, "in Gaza?"

"So what's new in art?" Frank asks, handing me a pair of chopsticks.

"The money's drying up," I say. "Some citizens in a small

city in Kansas are objecting to government funds being used for new toilet seats in the only theater they have. They would rather the funds went directly into crayola research for kindergartners, or into a program designed to aid policemen who've lost their ideals on the job and require firearms replacement. I understand their objections: why pay for private backsides with public money? The taxpayer wants observable value for his/her money. Anyway, why can't people just squat over the bowls without actually sitting? Do you realize how much money the NEA could save if toilets had no seats. And think of the thigh strengthening effect. I mean, whatever happened to the leaf-filled hole in the earth? This proposed toilet seat grant is the mistake of certain left of liberal, fastidious assholes in Congress who believe that what's wrong with the world is a lack of comfy padded toilet seats. Hey, this isn't England, where the Queen can't leave home without her own toilet seat. I think I'll write a letter."

"Julia, you're speeding, and we haven't even had our MSG yet," Frank says. Self-satisfied prig/pig that he is!

Kathy reminds me that the toilet seat controversy is a diversionary measure; the citizens' real objection is with a current play being produced there: a play in which homosexuality is alluded to.

"Oh yes," Jane says. "censorship by the hetero-masses is experiencing a rebirth in your country, isn't it."

"Shut up!" Juan says, "or I'll tell you about your country! Closet weenies, and shaved heads shoved up someone's bottom, a prince who fancies himself a bloody tampax at home in his sweetie's vagina, and a queen who set fire to her own castle by rubbing two royal pricks together."

"I've had enough!" Jane shrieks. "I'm getting out of here."

"You can't leave before the main course," I say.

"You're my guest."

"Fuck you Julia! You're as nutty as a fruit cake."

"Really?"

"Really."

"What makes you say that?"

"Because you are. You promised me a copy of the tape you made of me but you don't intend to deliver."

"I'll send it to England. I know how to mail packages to England. I'm not as dumb as you think."

"Okay then."

"While we're at it, why wasn't I invited to your book party? I read that it was a super blowout."

"I didn't have a book party. The publisher gave me a choice of putting the money into advertising, or having a party. Of course I chose advertising. "

"But I read about your party! Plimpton was there with his gang."

"It was another Jane. Not me. Maybe Jayne Ann Phillips, or Jane Doe. I feel sick! I was really looking forward to having a party."

Kathy says, "I think I'll order a side dish of bean sprouts, a side dish of eggplant, and a pot of green tea."

"Fuck you too," Jane says.

"Why me?"

"Because you and that new boyfriend of yours were fucking around in Julia's digs when she wasn't there. I saw you leave."

"Spy!"

"I happen to live there and I just happened to see you leave. I wasn't spying on you."

"This is great," Frank says, "Other people fight too. I'm so relieved. But I don't fight anymore. Juan and I have come to a new understanding. Nothing worth fighting about."

The waiter brings three large platters of food: dog ear, black, and oyster mushrooms with barley and soy beef, soy chicken with Fu-yu-tu pancakes dipped in egg-white froth, and brown basmati rice garnished with vegetables that have no name.

According to the rules of friendship, I thank Frank for having ordered exactly what I like to eat. I don't really care what I eat. I'm furious with Kathy (if it is true); how COULD she have entered my apartment when I was away! If it was Berkeley, California in the fifties, and the door was open, I'd understand it. Things were different then, but she was with someone she hardly knew! I know him better: that four-eyed detective, Flamingo. He and his partner have been making my life hell! Why haven't I asked them to show me their badges? Maybe I have. I can't remember.

"Kathy, is it true that you were in my apartment?"

"Yeah."

"Why?"

"Had to use the john, and we were in the neighborhood."

"How'd you get in?"

"Your landlord happened to be there, installing a light bulb in the hall."

"Was anyone with him?"

"A short white guy in green coveralls singing some Billie Holiday song."

"Does the light work? Did Stan fix it okay?"

"Sure. Bright as day now."

At this point I order a bottle of wine. I need a sedative to calm me.

During dessert (a tasteless red bean jelly with courtesy fortune cookies), Juan asks Frank, "Did you meet anyone?"

"I always meet someone," Frank answers.

"Were you careful?"

"I'm always careful."

"Is that all you have to say?"

"For now, yes."

They are looking daggers at each other.

"This is the year of the monkey," I say. "A time for hanging upside down by our tails. Says so on my informative paper placemat."

"This is the year of the leech," Juan says, "a time for bad blood."

Frank leaves.

Juan pays for the meal with his Mastercard.

I'm in a hurry to get home. Jane hails a cab. She thinks it will be faster than public transportation; however, there is an accident crosstown 23rd Street going East, and we are stuck in traffic till they clear it up. We have to drop Kathy off, too. On the way Kathy reports that the Abortion Project is off: (I'm glad I didn't tell her about my two abortions: the sons Josef wanted but will never have from me!). She's now working on Vas Deferens: a male thing. This I really can't identify with: heading sperm off at the pass.

The place is a mess: someone has been here. I take instant inventory to see if anything is missing.

My J.G.O. tape is gone. Even the one dimensional blowup of a cow that I had been planning to paste onto cardboard is gone, with all of my research material. I mean, this is too much. This is gonna cost me. No way I can do it again. Not even if Juvenal was here could I do it. I've lost the enthusiasm I once had for the project.

The letter from J.G.O. is still on the table. Might as well see what he has to say.

Dear Julia,

You have a great sense of humor. What makes you think I would pay you all that money? You ladrao! I don't care what the world knows about me. However, I will send you a portion of the money requested if you send me the master tape of my interview. Okay? You silly child, I would have sent you money for nothing. You did not have to threaten me. I like you. I will always like you. You accept me. You listen to my erotic stories and don't judge me. That's worth a lot isn't it. Expect a money order in the mail for the amount of five thousand dollars. After that it depends on whether or not I have received the tape.

Udderwise, all is well.

Yours,
Juvenal

P.S. PISSING, SQUATTING, PANTIES, SPURTING, FLOWING, BUTTOCKS, HOLE, LOINS, CHEEKS, DILDO, DICK, BOSOM,

125

PRICK, CLITORIS, THIGHS, FINGER, LOVE-LIPS, CUNT, WARM, MOIST, KISS, BREASTS, SUCK.   Adios
                                      J.G.O.

I'll have to stall him (pun intended); get the tape back somehow. But who has it? If I can't get it back I'll have to apply for the grant with my skeletons tape, or the one with Jane. As far as the skeleton tape, though, I really need the actual skeletons that were taken from me by the detectives (if they *are* detectives). Too much has been going on since I moved here; at least I'm no longer afraid of Josef. Maybe he's afraid of me. I'll have to ask him—cautiously, of course—otherwise he'd refute it. He hasn't asked me what refute means yet. I'm ready for him with that one. Whatever happens, at least I'll be receiving a five thousand dollar money order from Juvenal. That ought to tide me over till the next grant.

"It's so exciting here in the USA," Jane says. "We go out for a few hours and when we come back there's been a robbery. Are you sure they haven't stolen my interview tape too?"

"It's right here," I say.

"Good. I suppose it's not important enough to steal."

"I'm certain it has nothing to do with your intrinsic worth, Jane. It has to do with international intrigue, Percodan, cow-pats, pseudo-incest, steel, serial murder, lava baths in Kuaii, and acting."

"You know what I think?" she says.

"What?"

"I think your husband found out about Juvenal, took a bus trip here, and stole the tape out of jealousy."

"You might be right. And if he has the tape he's angry, and when he's angry, he's dangerous."

"So what are you going to do about it?"

"I'll call him and ask if he has it."

"Bad move."

"Yeah...because what if he doesn't."

"Call Marie. She knows every move he makes."

HE CAN'T GO FAR.

Marie says that Josef is in love with Clov and that he is going to ask me to divorce him so that he can devote himself to Clov (This is pretty far-fetched). I tell Marie that I will do so willingly if he returns a certain missing video tape to me. She says he hasn't been in the city since his incarceraton, and couldn't possibly have taken anything from my apartment, but she promises to concentrate on my dilemma. Marie has visions that reveal the whereabouts of missing persons and things: detectives use her to solve mysteries; dry cleaners to locate lost clothing; politicians to regain their lost ideals. When Josef was in her womb (she tells me) she knew he was a male child without having to resort to amniocentisis.

How was this revealed to her?

"I could hear the music of the spheres singing to me. Went like this:

> SHE
> (sings)
> LULU HAD A BABY
> HIS NAME WAS SUNNY JIM
> SHE PUT HIM IN A PISSPOT
> TO TEACH HIM HOW TO SWIM
> HE SWAM TO THE BOTTOM
> HE SWAM TO THE TOP
> AND WHEN HE WENT TO HIGH SCHOOL
> HE LOOKED LIKE IGGY POP."

If my eyes had been closed I'd have sworn it was Barbra Streis-DeBorscht singing her gushy heart out: Marie's voice is so earnestly nasal, so Hollywood schmaltzy—a side of her I'd never suspected.

She promises to cook me a birthday dinner using Northern Italian recipes that have been in her family for a number of generations, "Tagliolini all'orientale, involtini fra'cristoforo, patate purea, coste olio e limone, insalata, composta di frutta, vino: Rose Antinori."

I thank her for the offer, but say that my own mother has

something planned for me on that day. I have not seen, or heard from my mother since I left home.

FAMILY SECRETS

Q: What did you find in your father's handkerchief drawer?

A: Pills of all kinds: scattered—released from their clever child proof bottles by his aged hands, aluminum sealed pockets punched in one by one (seeking hurried relief from pain), empty plastic hollows that had once held medicinal lozenges (by prescription only). The acrid apothecary smell from beneath the drawer lining (where a sampling of fine powder had collected).

Q: And in the shirt drawer of his bureau, hidden beneath freshly ironed shirts?

A: Dirty pictures: a naked, sleeping woman on a couch, her legs lifted by a pair of anonymous hands to reveal her genitals; a foldout of Victorian pornography; a birds-eye view of a couple copulating in a field beside a car; my father in black socks, hiding his face (I recognize his nose) taking part in a daisy chain.

Q: Anything else?

A: In another large drawer, the fringed shawl he was buried in.

Q: Why did you go where you had no business going?

A: The attempt to decipher is natural to me. I require evidence.

Q: Is nothing sacred to you?

A: Everything is. However, do you suggest I worship at every shrine? Isn't it better to stand than to kneel? To keep ones eyes open. To speak one's fears rather than whisper them to some God who is hard of hearing?

Q: You seem to be on the defensive.

A: Wouldn't you be if you found out that your father was only human?

Q: Did you expect a God?

A: Someone to look up to. He was good to me, but he was

unkind to my mother. I can't forgive him for that. It messed
me up.

THE LADDER HAS MANY RUNGS

I look around for the ladder. I see it. I get up on the
ladder. I look out of the window on my right. I wipe the
pane with my sleeve. I Look. I Pause. I look again. (Just as
Clov did in my dream) Nothing. The street is underwater. A
bad day to go out. I have to go out anyway. I'm restless. I
don't take an umbrella. Let it rain on me! Do I want to get
sick and die?

WHEN FORTUNE SMILES
YOU CAN SEE THAT SHE HAS TEETH MISSING

"Your lucky numbers for the week, are: 7–14–19–26–
38–41," Marie says, "your father gave them to me for you.
He says you'll be a rich lady if you play Lotto Six next week."

"My father?"

"I was in the kitchen mixing pancake batter when he
visited me. Didn't float down or anything: shuffled in
wearing bedroom slippers, hands behind his back, shaking
his head up and down, then side to side. I thought he was
objecting to the recipe for pancake batter I was using, or my
utilization of rice bran oil instead of olive oil, but he had
other things on his mind."

"His mind? By the time he died he had no brain."

"You, his loving daughter, and the doctors in charge
of his case are entirely wrong on that account: your father
had a terrific brain, but it was flattened out, water logged.
Couldn't be seen with x-rays or other imaging machinery.
They should have given him a shunt to drain the liquids
into his stomach; however, that's neither here nor there,
since all's well that ends well."

"You think his life had a happy ending?"

"According to him, yes; rejoice, your beloved father is
in heaven and says it's everything he'd hoped for. He also

129

insists that he did leave the house to you. The papers to prove it can be found in a metal box beneath the highboy."

"What house? We couldn't even afford the rent on a one bedroom apartment, but he was pretty cagey about his money—mother found a hundred dollar bill hidden behind the radiator in the bedroom after he died."

"Also, the lady you asked about couldn't be found in heaven. She is still alive."

"I didn't ask about a lady."

"Her name is Nettie. She's ninety-five and lives in a rest home in Orlando."

"I don't know her, Marie. You're receiving messages for someone else."

"No, I'm absolutely sure they're for you. Your father hopes you will change your mind."

"About what?"

"He didn't say."

"Just like him."

"Your mother was there too, she says that her life is full and happy now."

"Mother...dead?"

"She really didn't mind leaving when she did. And she has her favorite nightgown with her, the one she thought the brassiere lady who came to her home, to fit her for a new bra, had stolen."

"Oh good!"

The case of the missing nightgown had really bothered me—almost as much as the vacuum parts missing story where she'd accused a neighbor of substituting plastic vacuum parts for her metal ones. "Never let anyone borrow your vacuum cleaner, Julia," she'd cautioned me, "or you'll end up owning nothing."

"That sailor you seduced on the beach in Miami," Julia continues, "says you should forget that terrible night and get on with your life. What is done is done and can't be changed. There is no point in dwelling in the past. It's time to move on. My nerves are shot Julia. I'm going to

Rosalyn Drexler

Maine to visit Josef and Clov."

MAL OJO

When things disappear, then reappear suddenly out of the blue, you can be sure there is a bad spirit loose in the world whose hellish assignment is to make a fool of you. After all the fuss and bother I've found the J.G.O. tape. Was it put under my pillow by the tooth fairy? (Tooth fairies are weird! What do they do with so many tiny baby teeth? Glue them to jewelry boxes as if they were decorative shells or rhinestones?)

I put the tape into the VCR; better check to see if it's been injured. Not a scratch—nothing till the end—and then—horribly—inexorably—a new ending unfolds—my film HAS been tampered with, has become a "snuff" film—with Juvenal as the victim. Is this Brazilian justice? Have the tables been turned by merciless assassins? Were they championing the rich or the poor? Certainly one or the other. That's what they have in Brazil: the rich and the poor: that's what Juvenal told me the day I interviewed him. Nothing inbetween unless one counts artists and writers. How clever of me to have cashed Juvenal's money order immediately. Mother would have called it "blood money." Well, if it is "blood money," I had nothing to do with opening the vein. I'm innocent. Ask Juvenal how steel liquifies to become the blood of his country, and why it only flows in and out of HIS pockets!

Someone else has it in for Juvenal. The evidence is playing itself out here, in the dark, in my basement studio.

SNUFF STUFF TUFF ENUFF
WHAT HAS BEEN ADDED TO MY VIDEO

At first I see an empty room. It is a well furnished bedroom with heavy, carved wooden furniture. A door opens. Juvenal is shoved into the room. His hands are tied behind his back, and he is wearing Calvin Klein shorts (fabric designed by Keith Haring: stick figures in shock); dirty Reebok Hexalites

131

ART DOES (NOT!) EXIST

(no socks) are on his feet. He is blindfolded and gagged. I draw
in my breath, shocked by what I see. This is not my work. I
realize that I can stop this horror by stopping the film, or I can
let it continue—I let it continue. There is a man on either side
of him. They are wearing panama hats and dark sunglasses.
Their suits are pale as silk pongee and look to be expensive. At
an agreed upon signal (the man wearing glasses says, "Now!")
they draw small, sharp, Swiss knives from behind their ears
(where they have been taped) and attack Juvenal with them.
He bleeds from the chest, the arms, the legs, the neck.

"Die you dog!" the man with good eyesight says.

Blood spurts everywhere.

The men place him on the bed face down; the bedspread
fabric is replete with black and blue flowers printed serially
upon a neutral tan ground; suddenly there are rosebuds and
cherries too: Juvenal's body is painting itself in blood. If I were
a botanist, I'd name a rose after him.

"Fuck it, he's ruin'n my new suit," the man in eyeglasses
says. He rubs at the bloody stain with his handkerchief. It only
spreads the stain.

"Who gives a damn anyway about your suit. Let's get this
job over with. Julia depends on us."

My name? Why would my name be mentioned? Is this
part of the Witness Protection Program I'm in? Was Juvenal
out gunning for me? And are these two fellows the infamous
Hawaiian Shirt Bros. who want to protect me until they get the
goods on me? What have I done? Hey I'm not only NOT
Kerouac, I'm NOT Franz Kafka.

These dapper guys (who couldn't be taller than five-foot
three-inches apiece), unzip their pants letting them drop to
the floor; then to be fair, flip a coin to choose who will be first
to sodomize the corpse.

This is certainly not my choreography. I would have
eliminated the coin flip and cut to the action. Storytelling is
what it's all about. You flip a coin, it interrupts the flow.

"You go first you dumb fuck," the irate loser declares.

The man wearing thick eyeglasses wins. He removes

them (a thoughtful gesture), hands them to his companion for safekeeping till he is done. "Don't drop them," he cautions, "or you'll pay for it."

"I'll be extra careful," the man replies. "Sure you can see without 'em?"

"I can see enough," comes the answer.

When he is finished, he retrieves his glasses, cleans them with a lens cloth, SIGHT SAVERS Brand. Puts them back on; turns to observe his companion as he violates poor Juvenal.

After a brief respite, during which they visit the bathroom to wash, or to relieve themselves, the rapists return and once again the deceased Juvenal becomes **THE OBSCURED OBJECT OF DESIRE**—His mouth is forced open to to be used as a tunnel of love; he is straddled, pumped and jolted— They've been to this fun house before, or so it seems, because they know just how to handle the twists and turns of the ride: how to avoid the sharp teeth, get the tongue out of the way, watch out for the glottis, THE GUY WHO SPREADS THE VOCAL CHORDS WIDEST WINS THE PRIZE: A FREE RIDE NEXT VISIT!! They perform fellatio with an energy and vigor usually reserved for the living with the living. I'd be hard pressed to choose a winner. The film ends as a thick, milky substance coats the lens.

WHO WAS BEHIND THE CAMERA?

What am I supposed to do with this tape? Sound the alarm? Use it to win a grant? Nobody will believe it's an authentic document. I mean, nobody believed those porno movies of women being killed and fucked were real, did they? So what do I do now? Leave the country? Or wait for instructions?

PRESSURE

I'm so fucked up, so lonely, so scared, so fuckin' sex starved I'd sleep with Stan Baltimore if he asked me to. At least then I'd be in heaven for a short time without having had to die to get there. I used to have orgasms in my sleep. Isn't that the height of alienation! Engorgement -disengorgement. And your hands don't even smell. Not even that, lately. So, Stan, why don't you call? Come on, Stan, call me and let's argue. How's your sister, Stan? Perfecting her one-woman show? Or does she come with the territory? Stan, I want you to know that I've discovered the trap door in the closet. There's an UNDERPASS that leads to your digs, isn't there? I can feel your breath on my cheeks at night while I sleep. What're you chicken? Afraid to get into bed with me?

THERE IS TRUTH IN WHAT I SAY, BUT WHO CARES

"Hey Julia, they're opening a new D'Agostino's two blocks from here. Grand opening tonight: free cold cuts, soda, stars. Wanna come?" Stans asks, expecting me to refuse his offer.

"Sounds great. Pick me up at six."

"You got it...Hey, did I hear right, you are consenting to be in my formerly non compis mentis company?"

"Yeah, I was gonna go anyway—Taking your sister?"

"Naw. She hadda get back to Baltimore: finally landed a part in a production at Baltimore Center Stage; something by Wendy Forman-Fornes. You familiar? Famous playwright. Should be good. Notion plays a talking stone who is proficient in both Yiddish and Spanish. She talks her way to Cuba, and manages to start a revolution by rolling over and crushing Fidel Castro, who is blinded by a 200 Watt bare light bulb as he lays dying. It ends badly for Notion though, because instead of becoming a national hero, she is thrown into the ocean and sinks to the bottom, never to rise again. The part was made for her."

"I wish her luck," I say.

23

The deli department is decorated for a party. There are streamers and balloons, and fresh salads of all kinds set out on large platters. I put some of the shrimp salad beside the coldslaw and potato salad already on my plate.

"Won't be fresh by next week," I say. "What they do is plough the stuff on top back down into the middle."

"Good selection of bread, though."

"Hey, look who's here," Stan says.

Mr. Flamingo and Mr. Palm Trees are near the cheese counter piling their plates high with food. They see us and nod hello. What the fuck do they have to be so cheerful about? I have just seen them kill a friend of mine. They must be aware of it. Should I make a scene right here, in the supermarket? At least they returned the tape. Maybe it's better now than it was before. Perhaps with the edited version, which is so far-fetched, so vulgar and violent, I stand a better chance of catching the attention of my peers (the ones who sit in judgement on the arts committee, but whose vote depends upon a personal agenda or vendetta, and not on what is truly deserving of an award)—does political assassination happen to be the flavor of the week? Or is strident ethnicity the call to arms? Maybe things'll soften up and the subject of mothers who nurse their babies will take the prize. My problem may not be subject matter—I have a sneaking suspicion that I should get newer and better equipment: a few Mac's, CD Rom, the latest, the best—do it all. How, without the big bucks? It's Catch-22. Extensive/expensive equipment is needed to make art these days.

Over by the fruits and vegetables a man resembling Josef is examining a hydroponic lettuce in its plastic container. His companion, a guy in a Mohawk wearing roller blades, is smelling and squeezing a beefsteak tomato. God, he really knows how to select the best of the best (he should be working for the NEA, or the MacArthur, or the Rockefeller). Look at him! He's testing the carrots: tries to bend one, he can't; the damn thing is as stiff as a prick in Springtime. Satisfied, he drops the bunch into his basket; then he snaps a string bean, it's crisp enough for him, so he scoops a few handfulls into a soft plastic bag to go; the strawberries don't meet with his approval since they are soft and greyish: in a state of mild putrifaction. He dumps the entire box out beside the strawberry basket display as a warning to others. I have often taken a seemingly fresh box of strawberries home, only to find when I picked them over that I had to discard more than half of them.

"Ladies and gentlemen," a clerk wearing a spanking new tan apron, announces, "I'd like to introduce you to Mr. Schlumberger DeMenil the manager of your store. He'd like to welcome you to D'Agostino's—the store that's come a little closer to you, by popular demand."

Mr. Schlumberger DeMenil ascends a wooden platform created to display the day's specials. At the moment it is bare except for him. He takes a Balzacian pose before he speaks: "This is a great occasion for me folks," he begins, "as your D'Agostino store manager it gives me immense pleasure to welcome you here. If there is anything that you need, that pleases or displeases you, please feel free to come to me. Let me know what you want. We are here to please you, the customer. That will never change. Thank you. Now please be our guest: feel free to partake of the food and drink displayed on tables around the store, and remember that whatever you taste at our tables can be purchased during regular store hours: all salads and baked goods will be offered fresh daily, the choicest cuts of meat presented, and a broad selection of fruits and vegetables will always be available in your produce department. Thank you. Enjoy."

Stan, pressed by the crowd around us, is pressing himself into me, taking advantage of this opportunity to excite himself. It's kind of a nice feeling, his body against mine, but I wouldn't want him to know it. He thinks he's getting away with something. My eyes are on Josef—yes it is Josef(!)—who has his eyes on me. The man in roller blades (who has been consulting Josef on this purchase and that) is moving his cart to the checkout counter. I can't avoid greeting my husband; being introduced to his friend—could it be Clov? I'd imagined a more ordinary looking man, old-fashioned, in a shiny gray suit, wearing brown oxfords—shy to the point of being obsequious. But this character with Josef is hardly servile. He watches the checkout clerk like a hawk; interrupts him to point out a discrepancy in price—the clerk acknowledges his mistake—yes, the item is on sale—he subtracts the price entered, taps in the correct price. The purchases are double-bagged and handed to Josef and his friend.

> THE COAST IS CLEAR
> AND THE HORIZON?
> THE SAME.
> CAN'T BE, MY PAPER BOAT IS STILL AFLOAT.
> ISN'T—I SUNK IT.
> IT IS WHITE—SEE THERE?
> I SUNK IT.
> IT HAS A SAIL TO CATCH THE WIND.
> NOT ANYMORE.
> BUT WHY?
> IT WAS YOUR PAPER BOAT.

A GATHERING

Josef, Clov, Marie, Stan, and the two detectives have dropped in for a visit after the opening.

"I'm in love with your wife," Stan declares.

Josef hands him a terrific blow to the midriff. Stan can't get his breath. He is gasping.

"Nobody's in love with my wife," Josef says, "unless I give 'em the go ahead, see?"

"I hate you!" Stan shreiks on gaining his breath. "I hate you!" He sounds like a woman who has no defense but the high-pitched screech of her voice.

"Now that's more like it," Josef declares.

"Aren't you going to introduce me?" his friend in the Mohawk hairdo inquires.

"Everybody—this is Clov. He's the top; he's the Eiffel tower."

"Unless I'm a crablouse," he offers sardonically.

Everyone laughs. Nobody knows what the hell he means.

"If you're a crablouse, I'll go get the powder, put you out of your misery," I say.

"She'll insecticide you to hell and back," Mr. Palm Trees declares. "Right?"

He waits for a response from Mr. Flamingo. "She'll let you have it," he says.

"You bastard!" Clov threatens the two detectives not knowing that they are authentic keepers of the peace and detectives first-class here to guard me from harm.

"This way. This way out," Stan whispers to Clov, directing him to the closet trapdoor. I see what he's trying to pull off. He wants to get me alone. One way to do this is to usher my guests into the closet and out through the secret tunnel that leads to his own apartment.

"This is terrible," Marie says. "Someone is approaching. Quiet everyone; an unwelcome visitor is about to enter!"

I am the unwelcome visitor.

I enter my fantasy. I exit my fantasy. I return to the real world: my work.

JUVENAL RETURNS

The wheelchair creaks. I tiptoe into the living room to have a look. I am carrying a loaded water pistol just in case.

"Over here," a voice instructs, "beside the ladder."

"Who are you?"

"Juvenal, your friend. As you can see I'm back."

"From the dead?"

"You seem rather nervous."

"I saw you murdered. It was on tape. The most odious things happened to you."

"Were you sorry for me?"

"I was overcome with grief."

"Thank you. It was only a ruse to make you feel something for me."

I am at a loss for words.

He continues: "One has to die in order to elicit strong emotions in others. I paid one of your friends to produce the little playlet at the end of your videotape. He was most compliant."

I am now able to see him. He is seated in the wheelchair, naked as the day he was born. He is a slight man, hairless, with a recent scar drawn across his chest, left to right. His penis is serenely settled between narrow thighs; and his elegant legs are crossed at the ankles.

"Will you have sexual relations with me?" he asks. "I can be very lovable—even entertaining if you'll let me."

"No, I won't."

"What would you do in my place?"

"I wouldn't have come here in the middle of the night to sit in a wheelchair with my clothes off."

"I couldn't help myself."

"Liar."

"Don't you need a patron?"

"I suppose so."

"Do you think I'm mad?"

"Wouldn't surprise me."

"Come here. If you make yourself available to me you'll have nothing to worry about for the rest of your life. I'm a wealthy man."

"How wealthy?"

"Wealthy enough."

"I was only kidding in the letter when I asked you for twenty million dollars."

"If you asked me, you meant it."

"Okay, I meant it, but I never expected to get it."

"I'm crazy enough to settle a huge amount of money on you: enough to subsidize your husband's Mickey Mouse experiments; enough to set you up with the latest equipment to produce your video installations, or whatever you call them."

"I can't."

"Don't be a fool—do you want me to eliminate you?"

"Kill me?"

"No, eliminate you—from the competition. I'm an influential man—I know people in your government."

"Nice of you."

"Take your time."

I walk towards him. If I can get behind the chair I intend to dump him on the floor. What then? Stomp him to death?

"I've made my decision."

"Good."

"What do you want me to do—sexually speaking."

His penis rises, nods in my direction, yet remains silent.

"Ask him," Juvenal says. "He'll talk if you coax him."

JULIA'S SCRIPT

CLOSE-UP OF THE PENIS. I AM HOLDING IT. JUVENALS' LIPS ARE ABOUT TO TOUCH MINE. HE DRAWS AWAY AND BEGINS TO STARE AT SOMETHING WITH INTENSE CONCENTRATION. HE IS FACNG THE CAMERA; MY BACK IS ALMOST TURNED TO CAMERA. CLOSE-UP OF JUVENAL'S BARE FOOT. ITS BIG TOE IS IN THE FOREGROUND.
I LOOK ROUND, THEN LOOK BACK AT JUVENAL. HE HUSHES ME, AND GOES ON STARING AT HIS FOOT. HE SLOWLY EMERGES FROM HIS PECULIAR TRANCE, SHAKES HIS HEAD, THEN GIVES A HELPLESS GROAN OF DESPAIR.
A STRING QUARTET PLAYS.

THE MUSIC GROWS LOUDER.
I TUMBLE JUVENAL FROM THE WHEELCHAIR.
WE STRUGGLE TOGETHER ON THE LINOLEUM FLOOR.
MEDIUM CLOSE-UP, TILTING SLIGHTLY DOWNWARDS,
OF US, I ALMOST FACE THE CAMERA. JUVENAL IS SUCK-
ING MY BREASTS. HE IS MOOING LIKE A COW. MY EYES
ARE HALF CLOSED, THEN OPENING THEM, ECSTATIC.

USEFUL WORD

"Hello."

UNPLEASANT REPLY

"Hello yourself!"

24

The Whitney wants a recent work from me for its annual celebration of *what's hot*, or *what's not hot* in a big way. I have nothing that's really right for them. The curator wants to visit my studio. Make a choice. Let her come. I've learned to never prejudge the judges. You can't know what the hell they really want, or are thinking (neither do they). They come to the artist for ideas. The artist with the best palaver, the most convincing air of seriousness, the most obvious connection to others working in the same vein (creating a school or direction: rather like a blindfolded prick fucking its way through a synchronized chorus of fur-lined cups), is the one who will be taken seriously, who will be given shows, who will be taken up and sent around the world to represent us, the USA, in all its trendy splendor and smut.

"Hello." The curator is here.

She extends her hand. When I accept the handshake, I am sickened: she does not receive my hand warmly. There is no squeeze or welcoming pressure. It is one of those hands that lies there like a "lox." (Lox: a salmon cured in a smokehouse till it lies on its side, boneless and passive.) This is a woman who chose, actually chose, to live her professional life with art! This repressed, withheld creature. (Perhaps I'm being too hard on her. How could I surmise all of this from a handshake?)

"Hello yourself," I reply.

"Juan Ferra told us about you. I don't know how we could have overlooked you, but there's still time to get you into the catalog."

"Yeah, well it happens." I mean to sound good-natured.

"All the time," she adds, shaking her head.

"Artists get lost in the shuffle," I say. A sore point with me.

"True. But that doesn't stop us from trying our best."

She's looking around. Doesn't know where to put her things.

"Obviously your best isn't good enough." I have the enemy in my sights and I mean to bring her down. This is known as cutting off your nose to spite your face.

She is visibly miffed.

Does she really think that her best is good enough? She smiles, trying to make the best of an unpleasant visit. Finds the table in the alcove. Puts her bag and umbrella down. Maybe I've won Brownie points with her—authentic artists are a pain in the ass—how often do you meet an authentic artist?

"Juan mentioned something about a mixed media excursion into the macabre," breathlessly delivered, as if the macabre were something she'd been searching for all her life. "We're interested in the surreal, the religious—totems of modern life—vestiges of the ancient."

"Mixed Medea," I correct her.

"Come again?..."

"Wordplay. You know Media/Medea. When an artist is rejected or ignored, she's liable to seek revenge."

She edges away from me. Not sure what I have in mind.

"Medea killed her children and fed them to her unfaithful husband. I don't get the analogy," she says.

She has an unpleasant nasal intonation.

"The children were what her husband valued and loved more than anything in the world. If it was a snail he valued, she'd have served him the snail. Anger and jealousy are stronger than love. Any kind of love."

She is determined to stay on course with me. "The Skeleton tape Juan told us about; are they skeletons of children? Real children?" She totally misunderstands what I've been saying. She might even think I'm a murderer.

"Naw, my skeletons are closer to gerontology than pediatrics. I'll get the tape going; you'll see. Would you like something to drink first?"

I hate offering collectors, curators, or columnists, refreshments as if I were some mendicant hostess buying their goodwill: yet I always have cheese and crackers, fruit in a bowl, and diet soda to offer. Can't shake my upbringing. The ugly niceness! The niceness unto death. The niceness that is subterfuge.

"Just some water, please."

"You've got it." I'm relieved.

Serving water is okay. A glass of water does not demand preparation, forethought. It comes out of the tap, or a bottle. A real artist may serve a glass of water without losing face. A real female artist may serve a glass of water without being perceived as having no fire! I hand her the glass of water without wiping the outside of the glass dry. Not thinking of that sort of thing is typical of a real artist.

"I have no napkins," I say. "Use the edge of the tablecloth."

She looks at her watch. It's a Swatch, one of those collector's items whose worth lies in its "limited edition" status and not in its ability to tell time. As a matter of fact, it has stopped.

"Gotta get a new battery," she says. "Could you tell me what time it is? I have another appointment at two."

"It's two now," I say.

"If it is I'll kill myself," she says.

"You won't have to. I was just kidding. It's twelve thirty."

A touch of sadism in this kidding around. Should she misinterpret the work, I've already wounded her. Cruel Julia. Is this the way you get the upper hand? How silly.

She sits in the wheelchair: a fun thing to do if it's not your only means of getting around.

The wheelchair squeeks pitifully, hoping to embarrass me in front of my visitor: I hardly need to be reminded that I have neglected it: rags and oil wait in the cabinet below the sink.

I toss her a small pillow for her back: the chair tends to make one ache after the first fifteen minutes of sitting.

"I'll explain later, if it's necessary," I say. "Please feel free to ask me anything. This is a work in progress."

She nods. I've got her where I want her. She'd nod at anything I say. My hostility is established. She knows that she has to avoid trouble. What she doesn't know is that I have, at this very moment, decided that all of my work, now and in the future, will be known as work in progress—unfinished—open to change—shifting and resistant to interpretation.

Lights out. Wait? Okay. Pause. Lights out.

THE SHOW BEGINS

SKELETONS reclining on
black velvet.
Single spot on one, then
the other as each
speaks.

SKELETON 1
Clov has signed a peace pact.

SKELETON 2
With who?

SKELETON 1
With whom.

SKELETON 2
Yes. If you say so; with whom?

SKELETON 1
With our son, Hamm.

SKELETON 2
God bless him.

SKELETON 1
It's about time. Hamm is dead.

SKELETON 2
Oh...How did it happen?

SKELETON 1
Broken neck. His scarf caught in
the wheel of that motorized chair
medicaid gave him.

SKELETON 2
Just like that dancer.

SKELETON 1
What dancer?

SKELETON 2
The one who believed in free
love.

SKELETON 1
Was she pretty?

SKELETON 2
Rodin thought so. She posed for him.

SKELETON 1
Oh, was she The Thinker?

SKELETON 2
She had some thoughts no doubt, but
not in marble.

SKELETON 1
Hamm was not a good man. I, his mother,
must finally speak the truth.

SKELETON 2
He was a sadist. It hurts me as a

father to agree with you.

SKELETON 1
The truth is the truth. He took great
pleasure in hurting others.

SKELETON 2
Found his masochist. Found his
helpmate.

SKELETON 1
Put him in a pumpkin shell.

SKELETON 2
And there he kept him very well.

SKELETON 1
Where is Clov now?

SKELETON 2
Up in Maine. Working as research
assistant to a doctor Josef Konrad.
They hope to find a cure for
NOMEATONTHEBONE.

SKELETON 1
No escaping it: one day the picture of
health, the next NOMEATONTHEBONE!

SKELETON 2
Hamm almost died of it. Remember how it started,
with bursitus of the shoulder?

SKELETON 1
Then he had that pain in his pelvis—bad teeth—
peripheral vision gone—boils—one thing after
another. So unexpected, to outlive one's child.

147

SKELETON 2
No cards of condolence can compensate...

SKELETON 1
Nor any memorial service bring back
the sound of his voice...

SKELETON 2
His touch as he shoved me—out of sight!
I'm crying. Forgive me for spoiling
your day.

SKELETON 1
No excuses, just stop your blubbering. I'll not
have it! Besides I have good news for you;
we are finally to be put to rest.

SKELETON 2
Will we have simple flowers carved
on our headstones, like the ones Mary Frank
carved for Jan Mueller's grave?

SKELETON 1
We are to be kept in a huge, temperature
controlled tomb called a museum, where we
will have many visitors to amuse with stories
of our living death and the death to come.

NARRATOR

CONTEXT IS, MAY BE, OR IS NOT EVERYTHING. A SKEL-
ETON MAY BE, COULD, SHOULD, OR IS FOUND AT
MEDICAL SCHOOLS, HALLOWEEN PARTIES, GRAVES,
MOVIES, MUSEUMS. THEY ARE LIFE'S READY-MADES:
THE HOUSE YOU CAN'T AFFORD TO PASS UP. AND CAN
THEY DANCE AT FIESTAS!
PULL THE INVISIBLE STRING BABY!

THEY DANCE.
THEY DANCE FOR HALF AN HOUR AT A TIME
SHAKING THEM BONY LEGS.
I'M NO FOOL. WHY YOU PULLIN' MY STRING? TELL ME,
WHO IS THAT MAN OFF TO THE SIDE WITH HIS HAND IN
HIS POCKET? CAN HE BE THE BIG, STRING-JERKING
SHILL HIRED FOR THE JOB? GOD?...OH.
HE HAS RHYTHM.
HE SO GOOD YOU ALMOST BELIEVE
THE PAPER SKELETON'S ALIVE,
CAN DANCE ON ITS OWN,
ABOVE THE GROUND,
IN THE AIR WITHOUT LOSING A BEAT.

SKELETON 1 (cont'd)
(First Amusing Story)
First time I saw my bones was in a shoe store. The salesman put a pair of patent leather pumps on my tiny feet and led me to the X-ray machine: "Step up, little lady, and let's have a look-see at those feet." The machine showed that I had bones in my feet. It was exciting. But it was the flesh that hurt in the too small shoes. The X-ray machine didn't show that. And who knows what harm (unregulated) the rays did to my bones? I think the shoe store sold Indian Walk shoes because I was given an Indian headdress with red and blue feathers as a souvenir. As I remember it, Indians went barefoot, or wore moccasins. Their feet were tough and did not need salesmen to sell them a bill of goods.

During a break, I explain what I'll require for my coming show. The curator listens attentively...but cooly.
"I'll need a bank of TV monitors covering an entire wall."
"I see."
"Because I'll want to vary the images or have them all the same. Also, a big screen opposite for closeups: talking skull, and images of the war dead."
"What war?" Panic has taken hold. She is no longer cool.

Perhaps she dreads a budget deficit. War, even in retrospective mixed-media conceptual bits, is expensive.

"All wars are the same. Whatever has been documented. A body part, a bloody organ, a toy with human transplants. It can work. You'll see. Hardest part's the smell of gunpowder and blood. Rot's easy."

"Very interesting...however, this may be more than we bargained for, you see..." she drifts off into "YOU SEE" language, the sour apologetics of one who must keep important things from happening. She is afraid that the sound of bombs going off at the exhibit will disturb the neighborhood, and perhaps mask the sound of actual bombs going off...those that may be set by madmen with a grudge against art institutions. "We're at high risk," she says. "Security would have to be at a maximum."

"Only thing you have to watch out for is The Guerilla Gals," I say. "If you don't include enough women in the show."

She comes to life, some wellspring of humor tapped. "The Gorilla Gals'll back down once we bring out our full artillery," she says.

"And just what might that be?" I ask.

"Bananas!" she shrieks, shaking with laughter. It is embarrassing to watch. She thinks she's funny.

"Would you like me to explain the philosophical and mythological underpinnings of what you've just seen?" I ask.

"Go ahead," she says, "I'm listening."

I SPEAK ARTSPEAK

"IN CHILDHOOD, A DOLL IS INVESTED WITH MAGICAL POWERS. IT DOUBLES FOR THE CHILD: TAKES THE HEAT SO TO SPEAK. PROVIDES A SAFETY NET. IN RETURN IT RECEIVES THE CHILD'S LOYALTY AND LOVE. NOW WHAT IF THIS DOLL LOSES A LEG, AND IN TRUE SCI-FI FASHION IS REPLACED WITH ONE OF THE CHILD'S? WOULD THIS MAKE CRIPPLES OF THEM BOTH? OF COURSE. THIS IS EXPERIMENTATION WITHOUT A

CHANCE IN HELL OF SUCCEEDING. IT IS DANGER-
OUSLY SENTIMENTAL: BODY COLLAGE, NOT SCIENCE.
HOWEVER IT IS COLLAGE THAT ATTEMPTS TO CREATE
NEW MEANING WITHIN AN ACCEPTED CONTEXT. TAXI-
DERMY BE DAMNED. ORGAN TRANSPLANT FORGET IT.
COLLAGE HAS NO IMMEDIATE NEED FOR THE SKEL-
ETON, OR ANY DAMN BUNCH OF BONES. IT CARES ONLY
FOR APPEARANCE; SOMETHING THAT LOOKS LIKE
SOMETHING. NOW I, AS CHILD/ARTIST/SURGEON AM
WILLING TO TIE THE TOURNIQUET, INJECT THE NEEDLE,
REPLACE THE BONE: PLAY "LET'S PRETEND" WITH
REAL PAIN, REAL LOSS JUST AS IF I KNEW WHAT I WAS
DOING. ON AN EMOTIONAL LEVEL THERE'S A STRONG
CONNECTION BETWEEN THE REAL AND ITS CONTRIVED
DOUBLE. I'M TALKIN' SHARED EXPERIENCE. I'M TALKIN'
VINYL, LYCRA, AND FLESH. I'M TALKIN' SUBSTITU-
TION. I'M TALKIN' WHO CARES, I'M TALKIN' DOESN'T
MATTER ANYWAY. I'M TALKIN' BELIEF IN ONESELF FOR
NO DAMN REASON. I'M TALKIN' FOOL'S GOLD. I'M
TALKIN' RED. I'M TALKIN' BLOOD."

"Um—sure—There's a dichotomy. But what you've just
shown me is a pair of talking skeletons who remind me, please
don't take offense, a little bit, of a play by Samuel Beckett," she
says.

"Right! So as we watch these mechanically manipu-
lated skeletons on all of these screens, we have an actual
cadaver being flayed on a gurney, in a transparent white
tent, by a medical student wearing sterile medical garb.
And, get this! He is laughing at his own jokes. I've wondered
whether using a laugh track would be putting it on a bit too
thick."

"You're the artist."

"The doctor is no different than a butcher. A side of beef
no different than a human body. In the end there's no pain
and nobody cries. The skeleton is life's logo. Who designed it?
Who the hell cares?"

"So you'll need a lot of space, that's obvious. And the sound system?"

I can't tell if she's on my side, or not.

"Yeah. Sound coming at you from every angle. Audio-vibrant-verity: macabre music, Mexican dance stuff, Rap, and people begging for their lives. We'll give out samples of Mexican candy, skull shapes, to the kids."

"Like a party?"

"A celebration of death, which is a celebration of life."

"This is more like an installation. I was led to believe it was a movie. Maybe we should wait for the next Biennial. See what you're up to then."

THE TRUTH IS NOT IN BONES, BUT IN SHAKIN' DEM BONES.

"I have movies too," I say lamely. I've really screwed myself...but have I?

"On second thought, I'll bring it up with my associates; maybe there's a way to get around it...." Giving me false hope.

"Thanks, then we'll be in touch."

"Soon. Soon," she assures me. "Meanwhile, keep working."

The snotty bitch. What a stupid thing to say. Does she think I'll ever stop working? She might just as well have said "Have a good day," that's how stupid she is.

152

25

JOSEF IS NOT WITH CLOV

Clov is in Cornell Joint Diseases hospital. They have him in traction. The theory is that if his spine stretches, and none of the vertebrae touch each other or impinge on his nerves, he will eventually be able to sit down. I don't think it's worth the effort, he could lose what he's gained. The man is a champion skater. He doesn't have to sit down to do this. He must, of course, become almost horizontal as he races forward.

Name me one thing you can't do standing up! You can sleep eat piss shit make love write a letter see a movie take a trip shoot a piano player, anything—standing up. What's so wonderful about the horizontal position? Dead is horizontal.

POETRY IS VERTICAL

Okay, so Clov's moves are as useless as Hamm's—he is only trying to put off the inevitable—the end. I'm beginning to feel something for Clov...tenderness? Annoyance too. With him in the hospital what will Josef do for companionable assistance?

JOSEF CALLS

"There is a plethora of lugubrious scientists in Maine," Josef says. "File that under forensic."

"What do you want from me?" I ask. I'm apprehensive. What strange thing will he ask for now? He once asked for my passport; then dressed up to look like me. He'd intended to travel to Bellagio (Italy) disguised as Julia Maraini. However his plans changed. He went to Austin (Texas). Listened to the hoarse cacophony of lice ridden grackles as they sat in trees

Art Does (Not!) Exist

(outside of the university library); fought off the thousands of tiny flies that attack at dusk, and returned home, disappointed. He hadn't even stayed long enough to be issued a student identity card. He is a creature of impulse.

After a pause he answers, "Mutual regeneration—I love you Julia in spite of your weight problem which brings with it its own burden of engineering challenges."

"In such a place and in such a world, why would what I weigh carry any weight?"

"Try this on for size," he says in that nasty tone I've grown to identify him with, "if you want me back you'll have to get a king size bed."

"What's eatin' you?" I ask.

"A computer virus has wiped out all of my research. What am I supposed to do, go back to staining slides in a makeshift laboratory? I'd rather kill myself."

SAVED BY THE BELL

One might say that Josef has been saved by the bell, since unbeknownst to him, Clov preserved everything on a backup disk. According to Marie, *People Magazine* is finally doing a story on Josef and his brilliant research; violent personality rehabilitated is the hook. Childhood abuse, the spice. They might try to drag me into it as the long suffering wife who stood by her man. If a movie is to be made, I want to direct.

"I'm trying lipids next," Josef says. "Lipids go right to the lungs. No side effects. No lingering doubts. No sudden death the minute I turn my back. I'm working with people now. Give them some hope and they'll let you try anything. Forget mice."

artfab@mama.ed

I'VE HAD AN INCONSEQUENTIAL DREAM. MICE IN MY ROOM. A GIRL FEEDING THEM. I ASKED HER TO STOP FEEDING LES SOURIS SINCE I DID NOT WANT MICE IN MY

154

ROOM. I HAD LOTS OF IRONING TO DO. MY MAKEUP WAS LAID OUT ON THE BUREAU. I HAD FORGOTTEN TO STAND THE IRON UP. IT WAS FACE DOWN ON SOME CLOTHES. NOTHING BURNED SINCE THE DIAL WAS SET AT LOW. I UPPED IT TO STEAM AND CONTINUED IRONING. AS I IRONED I MADE PLANS TO BUY POISON TO SMEAR ALONG THE BASEBOARDS AND IN THE CORNERS OF MY ROOM, TO KILL THE MICE. THE GIRL TOOK PANCAKE MAKEUP AND A SPONGE WITH HER WHEN SHE LEFT. I ASKED FOR IT BACK. IT WAS HERS NOT MINE. IN FACT HER SPONGE WAS IN BETTER SHAPE THAN MINE. NEVERTHELESS, I LEC-TURED HER ON KLEPTOMANIA, BUT I DID NOT TELL HER THE STORY OF THE GIRL WHO STOLE A RED GARTER BELT FROM ME THAT I'D BOUGHT IN LONDON.

Once I stole an imported red garter belt from a lady whose house I cleaned every Wednesday for four hours, to put myself through school. My analyst cured me by treating the Klepto-mania as a form of Cannibalism that could only be relieved by vomiting. That's how I became Bulemic.

THERE WAS NO GIRL. I MADE IT UP.

26

STAN BALTIMORE MAKES GOOD ON A PROMISE

"Hey Julia..."

"Stan...How ya doin'?"

"I have something for you. Remember I promised to get you a table?"

"That was a hundred years ago, Stan. I'm using this folding picnic table I bought at Ikea. It's okay."

"You can fold it up and store it for future picnics, because I've found the original table, the one that used to be in your place; it was in the basement."

"Oh."

"I'll clean it up, polish it, and get it to you first thing tomorrow."

"Thanks, Stan."

"You'll be in tomorrow?"

"Yeah."

HE BRINGS

A ROUND WOODEN TABLE OF GENEROUS DIAMETER RESTING ON A SINGLE MASSIVE CONICAL FRUSTUM FILLING THE MIDDLE SPACE.

WHEN I EMPTY THE BOX OF FAMILY PHOTOS ONTO THE TABLE I NOTICE THAT EVERY PHOTOGRAPH OF MY MOTHER IS TORN: THE HEAD RIPPED OFF! THIS IS FATHER'S REVENGE. ONCE AGAIN I AM SENT INTO THE PAST ON A RIVER OF TEARS: THERE IS FRIGHTENING SLAUGHTER ON EACH SIDE OF ME AS FAR AS THE EYE CAN SEE: MY MOTHER BEHEADED, HER BODY HURLED LIKE GARBAGE INTO A PAPER RIVER OF SWIRLING FOR-

GET-ME-NOTS.
WITH THIS VIOLENT GESTURE MY FATHER HAD CLEARLY DEMONSTRATED THAT WITHIN HIM DWELT THE SOUL OF A KILLER.
(A SOUL THAT HAD HELD MOMMA'S SEVERED HEAD UP BY ONE OF ITS EARS, LAUGHING, BEFORE GIVING HER A FAREWELL KISS ON BOTH HER SHINY GRAY CHEEKS.)
WHY DO CHILDREN HAVE TO KNOW THESE THINGS?

27

ADOPT THIS DOG AT YOUR PERIL

Detective Palm Trees and Detective Flamingo hold the three-legged dog between them.

"This is not an ordinary dog," Palm Trees says.

"It was a repository for illegal substances," Flamingo explains. "When we cut it open we found at least three kees of coke inside. Some must have gotten between the cracks in your floorboards.... We're not ruling out your labial folds either."

I expect him to ask me to "open wide" so that he can examine me.

"I vacuum twice a week," I lie.

"Your vacuum cleaner must be the highest vacuum on the block, sister," Palm Trees says, cocky and sure of himself.

"I wouldn't know about any other vacuum cleaners."

"So who're you protecting?" Detective Flamingo asks suddenly, his face close to mine.

(Why is it that only in detective stories are people presumed to be protecting someone? Isn't there any love or loyalty in ordinary life? For instance, I've never been asked who I'm protecting by a teacher, friend, doctor, or busdriver. And yet this protection "racket" is central to my character. Who am I protecting, indeed!)

The unlocked door to my apartment opens and in skates Clov: a welcome interruption. He circles the room three times, knocks on the wall twice, then confronts the detectives.

"She's protecting me," he says, "but she's not aware of it. It was I, Clov, who stuffed that toy dog with cocaine, and I who stocked the medicine cabinet with Percodan. There is so much pain here in this underground chapel. Can't you feel it?" he pulls on his hair, which is already porcupine quills, upward. He is full of emotion.... "By the way, Julia, where is that Percodan I left here?"

"I got rid of it," I say. "It was outdated...Say, you've made a fast recovery, I thought you were still in the hospital."

"I'm all better. They fixed me good."

"You're under arrest," Detective Flamingo declares, snapping a pair of handcuffs around Clov's wrists.

"Where are you taking him?" I demand. "He's not a well man."

"Is it catching?" Detective Palm Trees asks, worried.

"She's only trying to confuse us," Detective Flamingo insists, pulling Clov along as if he were a pull-toy, "she's done it before."

"He is chronically poor and shy," I say. "Let him go."

"Ms. Maraini, I suppose you are ignorant of the fact that Clov here, belongs to a clandestine homosexual subculture begun in the year 1823 in Biedermeier Vienna," Detective Palm Trees says, "and what is more, his bohemian marginality signals not reticence, but stubborn independence. Didn't he leave his employer Hamm without warning?"

"No, not without warning!" Clov cries out. "He made me suffer too much! When he asked me whether he'd made me suffer too much, I finally admitted it, "Yes!" I said, "Yes!" I waited on him hand and foot till I was bent double; I needed the pain killer as much as he did, but he was the one got it."

"Why do I always have to hear the sad stories; where are the happy ones?" Detective Flamingo asks no one in particular.

"This man, this middle-aged man in rollerblades, is seriously skewed," Detective Palm Trees declares, "he is accessory to the crime of murder. One does not innocently stand by, while two old people who are unable to help themselves die of systematic neglect, without alerting the authorities."

"I hate the authorities," Clov hisses. "Their clubs come down heavy on the guilty and innocent alike. Besides, when one dies in old age it is usually considered to be a natural death.

Hamm told me that. He said that his parents died of old age: the line of demarcation being seventy-two; his parents were over eighty. Had a good run for their money. As for their trash can homes; a mere convenience. Couldn't have three wheelchairs deployed within the same small space. Bad gambit! That's the way accidents happen."

"Isn't there something you can say in your own defense?" I implore. If he goes to jail that will make, let's see how many friends arrested? There's Juan, Dick Gull (The Guy), my husband Josef...how many more?

"I cut two peepholes in their cans so that they could see the room when they got lonely. Sometimes one of 'em would poke a finger through the hole and I'd pat it nicely," Clov says. "Gave 'em a cheap thrill. The best kind of a thrill: tawdry, sneaky, illicit..."

Detective Flamingo breaks in: "You cut them peepholes so that the fleas could get in and make 'em itch, Fleameister Clov! Torture comes easy to you!"

"Recognize this dog?" Detective Palm Trees asks. He has been waiting impatiently to spring this question on Clov; the reason they are here: Narco squad on the move.

"Yes. I recognize the darling. He had no name when we adopted him, but then since we had to call him something, we named him Sam. Sam What Am. There's a poem in his honor. Goes like this:

OH MY NAME IS SAM
AND I DON'T GIVE A DAMN
I'D RATHER BE A DOGGY
THAN A POH WHITE MAN."

This is all the confirmation the detectives need to implicate Clov in an illegal drug operation: Sam (the Courier) is Clov's gimpy dog.

"A dog so soaked in coke you could die of an overdose by just inhaling the dust off his filthy furry coat," Palm Trees says, blowing his nose in a fluttery silk handkerchief.

They take Clov away. Maybe I'll never see him again.

As I lower myself into the wheelchair, I see a small box

on the seat (that was not there before) addressed to Josef Konrad. Clov has left the computer disks for me to deliver.

A NEWLY SPAWNED SOCIABLE GUY

Josef calls: "Clov says that you're holding the data disks for me. I'd like to get them as soon as possible," his tone civilized, reasonable...not apprehensive at all.

"Where are you now?" I ask. The sooner I get rid of the disks the safer I'll feel. I don't have his equanimity. I've been stung before when I least expected it.

"I'm across the street at the public phone," he answers. "I can come right over."

"Good."

WHAT HAPPENED?

An hour passes and he is still not here. I can't imagine what's happened.

Phone rings. It's Josef again.

"Met a friend of yours," he says, "name of Juvenal. We had a few beers, talked, and then guess what, another friend of yours bopped by, a fabric designer? Kept blabbing about having been wrongfully accused. We're on our way to McSorley's...What?"

"Didn't say anything," I say. "So you're not coming?"

"How about tomorrow? My stuff should be safe at your place till then. I just can't dump these guys; havin' such a good time," he says.

"Hey I thought you were totally weirded out concerning those disks."

"I was...Hey, I'll call you tomorrow...or in a coupla days."

"Shit!"

"There's this interview with *People Magazine*. Have to get that straightened out. Listen, um, do you happen to still love me?"

"What's the difference? Aren't you and Clov lovers?"

161

"Tell you the truth I haven't seen him since that D'Agostino's opening. I miss you. You used to be so scared of me. I liked that. I was in control."

"I thought you were going to kill me."

"Might have. Wanted to do someone in. Lucky for you it was Dwayne."

"Josef, I have great sympathy for you, but I don't think I love you."

"Bitch!" he bangs his phone into the receiver (before I can ask him for a divorce).

After he hangs up, the phone keeps ringing. I do not answer. Don't give a damn who it is. It's probably him.

A few minutes later I relent and pick up the phone. It's Marie.

"I'm in love," she says. "You won't believe with who."

"I'm ready to believe anything," I insist.

"That brave young roller blader with the stiff orange Mohawk: Clov."

"You're kidding! He was just arrested. I saw it with my own eyes. They cuffed him and took him away."

"Well he's at my place. He got away. Here, I'll let you talk to him."

"Hello, Julia."

It's him.

"Hello, Clov. How'd you get away?"

"I paid them off, sucked them off, and saw them off."

"That easy?"

"Yeah. Hey, this gal, Marie, Josef's mom, is the answer to every man's prayer. She's an older woman but she's not my mother. I love older women. Took me a lifetime to find that out. I thought I was mad for men, but I was only making the best of a bad thing. You ever been trapped?"

"More than once," said with empathy.

"Hold on a minute...Marie wants to say something."

NOBODY LOVES ME BUT MY MOTHER AND SHE COULD BE JIVING TOO

162

"Hello. Julia? It's Marie again. Isn't he wonderful? So outspoken and sexy: much nicer than Dwayne. I've ordered four pillows filled with feathers and duck-down from the Home Shopping Channel, and a four drawer bureau from Macy's for his clothes. He's here to stay."

"Hello, Julia, it's Clov again. Would you please ask Marie to introduce me to her doctor. I need a prescription for an under-the-counter drug."

"Hello, Julia, it's Marie. I heard him ask you, to ask me, to refer him to my physician. I certainly will!...By the way, have you heard from Josef? That boy of mine has a nasty habit of disappearing from my life just when I need him. I thought we'd established a new understanding."

"That boy of yours is doing just fine. He's on a get acquainted binge with two of my friends."

"Has he picked up the genetic info disks?" she sounds anxious.

"Not yet."

"Oh I hope he doesn't wait too long."

"He wants to do that *People Magazine* interview first."

"Do you think he'll say nice things about me?" she asks.

"I can't speak for him, Marie, but I don't see why not. You've always been a good mother...that is unless the men you were with drove you crazy. Right?"

"Julia, this is confidential; I blame myself for Josef's lifestyle of fear and revenge. Sometimes I'd protect him, but other times I'd be frightened myself and not know what to do. I wanted to leave Mr. Konrad. I really did. But I couldn't. Thank God he died."

"Then you're guilty of cowardice, not maliciousness."

"I should never have been born," she sounds like she means it.

"Any significant dreams lately Marie?" I ask.

"Who needs dreams when life is so dreamy," she answers.

28

Kathy's just gotten back from Hartford with an update on her Vas Deferens Project. Whatever she does lately is called a project. This enables her to ask embarrassing questions, take notes, try samples, sleep free at the homes of project sympathizers, and get her name in the local papers. I don't know what she's really, deeply interested in, she skips around so much. The way she involved herself in the reproductive angle has puzzled me: *making* babies, *not making* babies. She's the perfect protest person with her loud voice, garish makeup, and homemade painted signs. If you didn't know her you'd think she was nuts. All she really needs is a lover/handyman to sodder her pipes for her.

VAS DEFERENS: THE DEFERENT DUCT OF THE TESTIS WHICH TRANSPORTS THE SPERM FROM THE EPIDIDYMUS TO THE PENIS.

THE WIND SHIFTS

"I'm off the project," Kathy says. "There's new scientific evidence that men who tie their ducts are more likely to get cancer than others."

"God, all those men who had vasectomies!"

"Yeah, just so they could persuade some dishy woman to fuck 'em with the promise that they wouldn't get pregnant," she says.

"So what's next?" I ask.

"I'm looking into animal husbandry."

"Oh?"

"Some farms are using dangerous methods to increase milk production."

"Such as?"

"I'm not too clear on it yet, but there is talk of placing a human gene into the blood of cows."

"No shit!"

"Yeah, and pigs too. Like, so they can make pig blood acceptable to human beings, with no blood or body parts rejected."

THIS IS A DIRECTION MR. J.G.O. COULD GO IN. BE OF SOME USE TO HUMANITY. OR IS HE ONLY INTERESTED IN ANIMALS TO SATISFY HIS PERVERSIONS?

"Have you heard who's on the Arts Committee?" Now she's breathless with excitement. Can't wait to tell me who.

"An old flame who is jealous of your career."

"Him? He's on the committee? Damn, he'll screw me. People think he knows what he's talking about. They'll listen to him. He'll sway everyone. I'm fucked. Dammit! I was depending on that grant."

"Hey, HEY! You can't be sure of that. The work is great. You'll get a grant. It depends on the quality of the work."

"It depends on who you know and who knows you, Kathy. If the work is good, so much the better. I've been on these committees, sometimes it's subtle, but always it's friends trying to reward friends. God, I've worked so hard and the work isn't even done."

"Chill...it doesn't work out, we can collaborate on a project together. Fuck Eugene Lee."

"Who?"

"Eugene Lee."

"Who's he?"

"The guy on the committee you once had an affair with."

"Kathy! For Christ sakes, that was Eugene Onegin. He isn't even in the country anymore. Went back to his roots: to mother Russia."

"Sorry."

"I'm fuckin' relieved. Wow!"

"Good; because sometimes people you think are your friends aren't."

"Decipher that one for me please."

"Has Juan called you?" This is a mysterious question. She never asks about Juan unless he hasn't invited her to a party.

"Not recently. He's too busy preparing his show." Maybe he has called me. I just don't remember.

"Arne Glimsher is courting him. If he was your friend he'd put in a good word for you. You belong at Pace. Kiki Smith is at Pace. Gets her paper and scissors free. Great catalogs they put out. Great Hollywood contacts. Your money worries would be over."

"Kathy, why you trying to sow seeds of distrust in me; you know that Juan has to be in the gallery himself before he recommends me."

"He won't do diddley-squat for you. He's been bad mouthing you all over town."

"He has?"

"Yeah. Says you set fire to your own place. Pretty radical huh?"

"Yeah, he must be jealous of me...like maybe I'm in line to win a big award and he's not."

"Like what?"

"Beats me...something significant, obviously."

29

A SPOUSAL SUGGESTION

He is here, sitting on a straight backed chair, the fugitive disk on his lap. He seems younger, more at sea, not as ominous as in the past, or have I grown impervious to veiled threat?

"Julia, I know you need money so I've kept myself aware of possible job opportunities for you."

"Thanks."

"And just by chance, on the news, I heard that the Disney people were looking for a Rat Lady."

"What do you mean by that?"

"They need someone to stay in a coffin with live rats. It's a seasonal job. For Halloween only."

He's serious. He thinks I'm capable of lying in a coffin, for God knows how long, with rats crawling over me. Now I know he's mad. Does he really believe I'm in love with rodents too? In a way it's cute. Naive. Stupid. In a way he wants me to break down.

"Oh, I'll bet the job's already taken. I mean it's such a visible job, anything could happen. A talent scout might catch the act," I say.

"I could train the rats," he offers. "They'd be reliable performers. You wouldn't have to be afraid of them."

"Thanks, but no thanks. I'm gonna be rich on my own soon. Don't have to be no rat lady. No rat in the hat lady."

"Julia," he says angrily, "I could throw something at you!" Immediately, he does. The disk glances off my head. Josef is a very controlling son of a bitch which I had forgotten. I'd become too cocky.

"Ow! You bastard. You're not even a real scientist. You're ersatz! You're a fucked up wannabee." I'm holding a handkerchief to the cut on my forehead. It doesn't hurt, though. Not too much. I wonder what he's gonna do next? Is he gonna be contrite and apologize, or escalate to a point of no return?

He apologizes; he's sorry for the one-millionth time; hoping that this tender moment will convince me to trust him, and allow myself to be bitten to death by a pack of rats!

"You never appreciated me," he says. "I'm an important scientist, my work on ADA gene therapy is going to help great numbers of people."

"Help yourself," I say spitefully.

"I'm not sick," he replies seriously. "I don't have a brain tumor. You know, I'm sorry you have no respect for the rats and mice who are my friends. When I tested my method on them, tumors disappeared. It relies on the same mouse retroviral vector system used in ADA therapy."

Detectives Flamingo and Palm Trees burst out of the closet, surprizing both myself and Josef who, on seeing them, attempts to flee. Flamingo pushes him back onto the straight backed chair, and sits on him.

"You are the focus of an intense investigation, Mr. Konrad. According to the law, you do not own the rights to your clinical discoveries since you made them while under contract to Gen. Inc.. I must ask you to hand that disk over to Detective Flamingo who is seated on your lap," Palm Trees orders. He has a gun aimed at Josef's head.

Josef hands the disk to Flamingo with some difficulty, since he has to extract it from beneath his sitz fleisch.

"Also," Palm Trees declares, "Ms. Julia Maraini is under our protection until we get the goods on her; therefore, you are to stay away from your wife until such time as you are deemed to be reformed and sweet tempered."

"I understand," Josef says contritely, then pulls a long string of brightly colored words from his mouth as if they were a magician's cache of silk handkerchiefs:
"APHERESIS
INTRAVENOUS
INCUBATION
IMMUNE

ISOHEMAGGLUTININS
ENZYME
NORMAL
INFUSIONS
TOXINS
HEMOPHILIA."

The words overwhelm Josef. He is in their spell. Clearly Dwayne's death has released something in him. Call it language. Call it poetry. Call it a laundry list: the dark colors and the light, the heavily soiled and the barely used. The detectives don't give a shit for his brilliant progress. They've come to take him away. To them he's a thief, a wife beater, a kook.

Detective Flamingo, ignorant of science, yet full of passionate fervor, says, "I don't go along with this newfangled gene therapy. Don't think it's ethical to alter a genetic line for generations to come, Mr. Konrad...however, I'm the kind of guy willing to wait and see what happens. Benefits and drawbacks, still unclear. Right? No one will ever convince me I evolved from a can of fish bait."

As the three of them exit, I breathe a sigh of relief. "We'll be back," Flamingo assures me, "but till we do, keep your nose clean kid."

"Before you go," I say, "tell me this—Who filmed that porno film you were in?"

30

MARAINI DISCOVERED BY HERSELF

I admit that all along I was the person behind the camera. (Who else could it have been?) That I was the one who was paid to make a flic your bic, docu-fuku movie with Juvenal as the (victim) star. If you've ever wondered what to do with your money when you've got more than you'll ever need in this life—put yourself into your own movie fantasy. That's what Juvenal did—just like Hitler with Leni Reifenstahl, Juvenal bought himself the services of one of the world's best artists, me! And he's returned to Brazil a happy man. I'm sure I'll receive letters from him saying absolutely filthy things; not to worry, in a way I'm privileged to know him: such a sleaze, such a prime and glowing example of the lowest of the low. However, is he really the lowest of the low, or just another run of the mill guy with money to burn?

IT IS THROUGH ART THAT WE CAN UNDERSTAND OURSELVES AND REALIZE OUR POTENTIAL...

I'm leaning in the direction of the Skeleton installation. Death really hits home. The J.G.O. stuff is too foreign, too pornographic, and too long. Total time of presentation for all materials may not exceed 10 minutes. Them's the rules. Ten minutes is a joke. Will they get it or will they won't?

THROUGHOUT THE AGES, HUMANITY HAS STRIVEN TO GO BEYOND THE LIMITS OF THE IMMEDIATE PHYSICAL WORLD TO CREATE THAT WHICH WAS NOT THERE BEFORE AND THUS NOURISH THE HUMAN SPIRIT...

The Jane Birch material is not finished to my satisfaction: I'd have to go to Cambridge (England) for additional visuals, and I don't think the committee would be interested in a Cambridge travelog (said with tongue in cheek) that speaks to a little girl's anguish over her father's revelation that he is homosexual. Things have taken another turn here in America where happiness may be a set of golden cock rings, followed by a trip to Denmark for the wedding.

THE FIRST RECORD OF OUR PERCEPTION OF THE WORLD AROUND US WAS THROUGH ART SCRATCHED ON CAVE WALLS, CARVED ON STONE, OR MODELED IN CLAY...

The Guy material is pretty good, but I haven't had time to work on the sound or visuals. I should get in touch with Dick Gull (The Guy), see what the guy is up to. He's not as dumb as he makes himself out to be...and I might have him collaborate with me on some aspect of his own life; is it the real or is it the mock?

AND IT IS THROUGH ART THAT WE WILL BE REMEMBERED BY THOSE WHO WILL COME AFTER US...

Q: Are you going to give yourself up?
A: Have I committed a crime?
Q: Detectives Palm Trees and Flamingo have the goods on you.
A: Oh them! They're former actors who're on the advisory panel for the visual arts fellowships.
Q: Do you trust them?
A: They're the only game in town.
Q: What's next?
A: My application is complete, in the box, stamped and ready to go: I've edited the skeleton tape down to ten minutes.

It's not complete but this makes it better.

Q: What if you don't get it?

OUR NEED TO MAKE, EXPERIENCE, AND COMPREHEND ART IS AS PROFOUND AS THE NEED TO SPEAK...

A: There's always a next time, unless there isn't.

GOOD NEWS?

Juan always knows what's going on, so I believe him when he calls to say that Allison Arcadia, the Whitney curator who visited me, was no longer with the Whitney. "She had a breakdown," he says.

"God!" There goes my big contact.

"Yeah, she went paranoid in toto. Thinks people are out to get her. Didn't you notice her weird behavior?"

"I thought she was just a typical curator. What do I know?"

"They've replaced her with a recent Yale graduate who's crazy about your kind of stuff. Get ready for a powerful boost, kid. And by the by, he loves to receive tokens of respect from artists in the form of works of art."

"Give him something?"

"Feed the animals their preferred food."

"You got anything else to say that'll shake me to the roots of my being?"

"Nothing that directly affects you, but I have the latest word on Mr. Steve Drummond..."

"I thought he died."

"That was Steve Ross, not Steve Drummond. Mr. Drummond is the Director of the Whitney. To lure him from Boston in 1991 the Whitney board gave him housing costs, the cost of a car and driver, life insurance, the cost of sending his two brats to private schools, and a diamond tennis bracelet for his wife. His actual salary appears to stand at around $250,000."

"So what does he do for it?"

"He attracts money and art donations. It's hard work."

"Oh."

"Yeah, poor guy: it's a seven day week, with lots of entertaining in the evening."

"So what do I do about the Whitney biennial?"

"Sit tight. Allison turned her notes in, along with recommendations...now it's up to the committee and the new curator to get in touch with you."

"Juan..."

"Yes?"

"How'd you get the inside track?"

"I sleep around baby."

"Isn't that really retro-behavior? You wanna get a disease known globally by its three letter abbreviation?"

"HIV? Naw. I take precautions."

"Like what?"

"I ask 'em if they love me."

"How'd the benefit at White Columns go?"

"Raised something for research. Not enough."

"Tant pis!"

"French for what?"

"So much the worse."

"Someday I'm gonna study a language like French. I may have to go there if I get a show at the Beauborg or something."

"Yeah. Best to be prepared."

31

The new curator has come and gone, taking with him the diagrams and sketches for an installation (my gift to him). He is so enthusiastic it's scary. Makes me feel like disappearing. He not only wants me for that one shot at the Whitney, but promises he'll get me a retrospective within the next two years.

He also took with him a gift wrapped box of Turkish Delight that I bought on the lower East side. There is nothing in the world I love more than Turkish Delight, but it's hard to find. One must live with the times. One must develop new tastes: malt balls, gummies, bridge mix. There is a soothing effect on the gastro-intestinal tract when sweets are introduced.

I was really shaky when he left. I had resigned myself to the customary reaction followed by polite rejection...now this: further opportunity! Who knows how or why it happened! You dream, you work, you plan your life or death (on bad days), and you hate yourself (for sins only you know about), then the angel of mercy intervenes, tossing you a magic feather. What does one do with a magic feather(?), dip it in blood and write the Declaration of Independence according to Maraini? Hardly. You do what any self-respecting performance artist would do—you put that elegant feather right up your ass and do a funky chicken dance (pecking away at air, flapping your arms for takeoff): God's FOOL you ARE, and God's FOOL you BE.

artfab@mama.ed

Hello are you there Julia?
I'M HERE.
Sure you're not at EXIT ART?

SURE! WHY?
People living in their installations: side by side. Almost.
IT'S BEEN DONE BEFORE. NOW APPEARING DAILY UNDER
NOT-FOR-PROFIT AUSPICES OF THE HOMELESS.
Yeah, you're such a wise ass Julia. You don't see the difference
between art and
ARTERIOSCLEROSIS? HEY ART LOVER, YOU HEARD THE
ONE ABOUT THE ARTIST NOW BEING SPONSORED BY THE
NEWER MUSEUM? SHE IS MAKING A HELL OF A REP FOR
HERSELF BY TRAINING CHICKENS FROM EGG TO AIR, TO
FLY. THEY TRAVEL WITH HER TO "IMPORTANT" ART EXHI-
BITIONS ALL OVER THE WORLD AND WHEN THEY DON'T
PRODUCE SHE EATS 'EM FOR DINNER.
So what's your point?
I IDENTIFY WITH THE DELECTIBLE, EDIBLE CHICKEN WHO
CAN'T ESCAPE ITS FATE EVEN THOUGH IT'S A VIRTUOSIC
PERFORMER. MUCH AS I HATE TO ADMIT IT, THERE'S A
MILLION MORE LIKE ME WAITING IN THE CHICKEN WINGS.
Are you famous or something, Julia? Should I know you?
IS ANONYMOUS FAMOUS?

32

PREPARATIONS

What have I gotten myself into? The road to success is paved with vinyl, cardboard, wood, nails, glue, and broken objects. I'm tormented unnecessarily by myself, as if presenting my work to the public is an act more demeaning than taking a crap in the street. I don't like this side of me. I've got to learn to stand on sturdier legs. To welcome the good life. Henceforth, I promise to banish negativity...to be frivolously joyous.

Mr. Palm Trees and Mr. Flamingo who are no longer detectives, or shooters, or actors, or arts panelists are helping me get things together. They have turned over a new leaf fashionwise and wear jeans and blue work shirts as is only proper in an artist's studio. Marie drops by once in a while with a lemon nut cake, or strawberry shortcake from Dean & DeLucas. We drink strong Columbian coffee instead of tea, while she complains to me about Clov, who is, she says, promiscuous. I stop myself from reminding her that Clov has been translated into many languages, and that people all over the world know him intimately (even her son Josef, my husband!). I tell her, "One must respect a new lover's past; his life is his life, and your fiction regarding him, is your fiction." She nods in agreement.

33

SHE WHO WAS HE

Kathy BienSur shares her K.D. Lang tapes with me. She's in love with K.D. the way I'm in love with Hatshepsut, who was a female Pharoah: "She exhales the odors of the divine dew, her fragrance reaches as far as Punt,it mingles with the odors of Punt, her skin is like kneaded gold, and her face shines like stars in a festal hall," say I. Both ladies hide/hid their femaleness behind traditionaly decorous rainment (reserved for the male sex). Powerful personages. Kathy is on the right track at last. If only she'd remove those nostril rings. What does she do when she has a cold?

IT DOESN'T RAIN BUT IT POURS

The NEA grant has come through: it's overload. I'm too lucky. How can I come to terms with my guilt? But I do! I do! How many undeserving freaks collect small fortunes from big foundations? Do they suffer because of it? Never. They take the money and run. Besides I'll need it to complete my work— a piece I'm evolving: Outer Space Antic Theater using laser light (thanks to Wilson) to deconstruct a Newt Fornes play based on Moliere. I would like to collaborate with Dick Gull (The Guy) when he gets out of jail because I see this piece as all design: costume, light, movement. It makes me really happy to take multi-media so far away from serious contemporary concerns.

34

AS REPORTED IN THE STAR

JOSEF'S GIRL
Although genetic scientist JOSEF KONRAD
claimed recently that his relationship
with artist JULIA MARAINI was kaput, he
is once again dating his former wife. A
source close to his family tells us that
Maraini recently spent a week in
Maine with Konrad, before heading
off for a sojourn in Brazil, where she
intends to spend part of her NEA grant on
research for a new project.

Meanwhile, Konrad has turned to his
close friend and confidant CLOV for
companionship. We hear that Konrad's mom
MARIE KONRAD (of "Stop him! Stop him!" fame)
has arranged for a double wedding when Maraini
returns. One source says, "She is in love with
Clov, and can't wait for them to tie the knot."
Konrad lives in fear that his mother will
disinherit him if ever she discovers him on the
town or in the townhouse with pal Clov.

If Marie Konrad decides to sue her own son
for alienation of affection, you can bet that
Liz Taylor, a recent but devoted friend
will hobble to his side to comfort him.

In a slightly different spin on the
story, an old character who goes by the name
of Hamm reports that he is trying to work out
an amicable arrangement with Clov, Josef,

and Marie. His prominent display of a buck
naked derrière while being interviewed by
reporters, caused quite a minor uproar among them.
But he declared that he is ready to forge
ahead with his plans for more nudity, if his
demands are not met.

35

THE FRUITS OF MY LABOR

I'm buying a condo on the upper East side with a terrace and two bathrooms. Wouldn't have been able to do this with my award money alone, but Josef is cashing in on his new discoveries. Everyone is beating a path to his door: offering him money, equipment, laboratory space! I've been looking for a studio too: something really big, maybe 3,500 square feet in Tribeca. In a way, being recognized is a pain in the ass: just yesterday as I was walking down the street with Josef, someone rushed over to me and grabbed my sleeve, "Are you Julia Maraini?" I said yes. Then the person turned to her companions and said, "See, I told you so."

My fifteen minutes of fame: an article in *People Magazine*, an appearance on the Donahue Show, has brought me this, a total stranger stopping me on the street for no good reason. Josef has to wear a knitted cap pulled down over his forehead, and a navy pea coat, so that he won't be recognized; however, a few people have chased after him anyway thinking he was Al Pacino.

36

FAME AND HOW I AM PERCEIVED—
THE WAY IT REALLY IS

The following article has recently appeared in the Sunday "Arts & Leisure" section of the *New York Times*.

****

CELEBRATED ARTIST MARAINI CELEBRATED

In one of her rare appearances on film, the artist Julia Maraini (known to her friends as Ma) defined the artistic dilemma: "There is nothing new to express, nothing new with which to express it, no desire to express something new, therefor why not recycle what has already been expressed?" In this instance, Maraini was speaking about the predicament of young artists today, but her words may be applied to her own work which appropriates without apogee, the entire history of art. Ineluctably drawn to her destiny, Ms. Maraini celebrates the achievements of others in a more modest mode, her own, for which she is rightfully (or wrongfully) rewarded in the marketplace...a marketplace heretofore unmatched in its voracity for the chic, the overpriced, the hollow: "If it's hollow, it's my job to fill it," Maraini confided to this reporter. And fill it she has! As we celebrate her 24th birthday, it is evident to us that Julia Maraini is the preeminent artist of her time: 1994 to 1995 and one-half.

****

The themes that have preoccupied her for more than five years, pre-dating her use of them in her work, instills all of her work, and, one might add, her waking and dreaming hours.

Indeed in one highly publicized experiment, Ms. Maraini lent herself to a sleep disorders laboratory so that the electrical

181

impulses of her brain while asleep might create an artful graph, later used as the theme of her powerfully evocative show: THE DREAM IMPULSE AS GRAPH.

"This is as minimal as I'll ever get," she said. "Call it an aberration if you will; I prefer dreaming to graphing." At 24, she is both an icon of her age and an emblem of the 'Get it while it's HOT!' generation. If she can go on, perhaps we can follow.

****

On her birthday, May 22nd, she will be honored throughout the world. This week in New York, almost daily lectures and panels have been analyzing her art. In London, there will be a major retrospective of her work as well as a four day symposium. In Paris, Maraini specialists are already gathering to deliver papers as varied as (translation from the French), 'MARAINI AMOURINI' and 'THE PROLIX MOO-COW IN ITS RELATIONSHIP TO MARAINI'S MA-DADA HOOKUP.' Riot squads have been enlisted to keep the peace, since opposing factions of under-appreciated artists threaten to make trouble as is their wont. "I'm ready for 'em," the artist is reported to have said. "If they want trouble they've come to the right place." However, Maraini with her youthful high spirits detests anything that smacks of violence... although...her installation: BLOOD AND GUTS 1, deals with a grave and chilling subject—the C section upon a dead woman to remove her living eight-month-old fetus. Even at her most tragic there is a comic vein—a throbbing, unclogged viaduct that bubbles forth unexpectedly whether she is speaking to a critic, or mixing her metaphors at a purely social event: "The pratfall, the pie-in-the-face, the banana-peel underfoot, the chalk-sock attack is meat for my grinder," she confides, "nothing's too low for me. I'd say that my influences have been the Ritz Brothers, the Marx Brothers, The Three Stooges, and Camille Paglia."

Rosalyn Drexler

****

The unfortunate thing about the irrepressible Maraini is her admitted addiction to the color cobalt blue...Is this her signature? "Oh no, I just happen to have a lot of cobalt blue around. It was on sale at Pearl Paints, so I stocked up. Cobalt blue is like having a little bit of heaven in a tube. Sometimes I get such a transcendental suito-religious feeling when I squeeze that color out of a tube, that I have to hold on to something. I once had an out-of-body experience because of cobalt blue...I left my body in the studio and traveled to Genoa, where I ate a hot sausage, pepper and onions sandwich before returning. Don't ask me how I did it. I juice did. When something works you don't question it."

****

If I have slighted the serious side of Julia Maraini's oeuvre, allow me to remedy that impression with another one: the artist appeared at her retrospective at the Whitney wearing a blindfold and carrying the scales of justice in one hand, a smoking revolver in the other. Impressive? Serious? Subversive? In a word, yes. Also familiar. Too, too familiar. She means to be. On the subject of other artists alive or dead, she has a bone to pick with Magritte. "It would have been much smarter of him if he had said, 'This IS a pipe,' instead of 'This is NOT a pipe.' If he had, there would have been a lot more excitement; people would have wondered why he bothered to say something that anyone could plainly see. As an example, why would I go around saying this is not a nose while pointing to my nose? If I went around saying this is a nose while pointing to my nose someone might get angry with me and punch me in the nose for thinking him stupid. As an artist I prefer the risk. A good punch in the nose validates one's sedition as an artist.

****

183

In JULIA MARAINI at 24/MARAINI out of CONTEXT, a Neo-Neoprene anthology of essays published this week, the critic Denise Furthiana refers to the increasing fragmentation and lack of a center in Maraini's middle-to-late works. She asks: "Is this fragmentation a negative point? Is it a reaction to university graduate art courses? Is it a reaction to the figurative neo-expressionism of the Germans, Italians, or Dutch? Is it a departure or an arrival? Who has the timetable?" Furthiana's discourse does nothing to relieve our curiosity. The questions remain unanswered. Perhaps posterity will discover the answers. Perhaps someone will think to ask the artist.

****

Just as the later works are being reevaluated, her earlier installations have achieved classic status. Her INTERVIEW SERIES 1 & 2, are among the most important works of this century and, I might venture, of centuries to come. Although not quite a matched pair they are unified as dramatic realizations of that decidedly undramatic subject, the job interview. "I wanted to paint chairs, and so I had to find a situation in which the use of chairs was a given. I was surprised to find that when these chairs were occupied by two figures an almost palpable tension was created between them," Ms. Maraini explains. What led her to do the series? "I've been interviewed and I've had to sit on hard chairs opposite very hard people. One job interview after another. It made me sick. The Interview Series really wiped me out, emotionally speaking. Have you ever been a job hunter? Have you ever been a cardboard cutout? Same thing."

****

Julia Maraini is in fact one of the most autobiographical of artists, pulling art from her own experience while concealing the source. At one time she had considered cutting out pieces of herself just as one clips photos from a magazine, in order to affix her flesh to photos of herself; on hearing that an Italian artist was involved in something of a similar nature—having plastic surgery done to her, in a gallery, with an audience present—Maraini dropped the idea. "I do not want to be compared to a rampant non-talent," Maraini says, "though who is competent enough to pass judgment on me or anyone else?" She claims that friends of like mind and activity are important to her: "I cannot emphasize enough the importance of socializing with people who are on your level, who are doing things, who understand your attitude, and who are willing to go out on a limb for you career-wise. We collect each other's art. Eat together. Dish the competition. It's reassuring. Sometimes, I think we're the only artists in the world who matter. I mean, who else is there? Who gives a damn?"

****

I honestly believe that Maraini has created a body of qwork that will insure her mortality (Note: the awarding to her of the Noblesse Oblige Prize for New Forms in Art in 1993).

Her work has liberated a whole new generation of artists from traditional concerns: in Germany there is Johann Phyrick Meistersinger and Helene Wurmsturm; in Italy, Salvatore Amici Con Brio, Piero Della Mortadella; and in America such painters as Sally Brotlett, Ski Boroff, Bobby Basket, and Spike Lowbide.

****

For someone whose reputation is that of a woman larger than life—a kind of forbidding East Side Valkyrie—she is surprisingly vulnerable and generous with her time. She remembers what it is like to be poor, unknown, and homeless. "I never knew where I'd sleep from one day to the next. I was hungry all the time. All I had to work with was an HB Venus drawing pencil, a blunt scissors, and an 8" X 11" sketchpad...then I met this nice lady, this gallery director who'd moved from Sixth Street and avenue C to SoHo. She took me under her wing with an umber of other local vermin, and I thrived." Conversation with Julia Maraini often ranges from her main interest, art, to sports: Japanese female wrestlers, rollerbladers; to astrology - she's a gemini: quirky, quixotic, as changeable as quicksilver; politics: Austria's ties to its Nazi past; science: the inadvertent destruction of the world through nuclear accident; and music: postmodern music as it relates to third wave bird calls.

****

As her 24th birthday approached, I sent her a letter raising the possibility that she might have something to say publicly about the millstone, her last year before achieving a quarter-of-a-century of living. Unsurprisingly—and politely—she replied that she still had a lot of living to do, God willing, but to ask her again in seventy-five years. I marked the date in my perpetual calendar.

****

Along with many others, I first encountered Maraini on a visit to her studio accompanied by a mutual friend. At that very moment I knew that I was dealing with an important person-age/artist/human-being. Her work astounded me. It was so strong that I immediately became nauseous and had to excuse myself. Brilliance affects me that way. I left the studio in admiration, sure that I had discovered a moving farce, a voice of strength proclaiming itself...a fascinating brilliant assertion of the complexities of the art hustle...a return to a romantic era...the new Bohemia. In two subsequent years my suspicions have been borne out; Julia Maraini is not only a contender in a heavily populated art scene, she is the art scene.

j.j. with R.S.

186

CORRECTIONS *

Please note editing mistakes made in yesterday's article on Julia Maraini. The incorrect word will appear first, followed by the correct word.

* apogee	apology
* suito	pseudo
* juice	just
* sedition	position
* qwork	work
* mortality	immortality
* an umber	a number
* millstone	milestone
* farce	force

THE END